Just J

Colin
Frizzell

ORCA BOOK PUBLISHERS

Library and Archives Canada Cataloguing in Publication

Frizzell, Colin, 1971-
Just J / written by Colin Frizzell.

ISBN-13: 978-1-55143-650-0
ISBN-10: 1-55143-650-7

I. Title.

PS8611.R59J88 2007   jC813'.6   C2006-906135-1

First published in the United States, 2007
Library of Congress Control Number: 2006937241

Summary: After her mother's death, thirteen-year-old Jenevieve deals with her grief, her father's neglect and her aunt's eccentricities.

Orca Book Publishers gratefully acknowledges the support for its publishing programs provided by the following agencies: the Government of Canada through the Book Publishing Industry Development Program and the Canada Council for the Arts, and the Province of British Columbia through the BC Arts Council and the Book Publishing Tax Credit.

Typesetting by Christine Toller
Cover artwork by Janie Jaehyun Park
Author photo by Nicki Roswell

Orca Book Publishers
PO Box 5626, Stn. B
Victoria, BC Canada
V8R 6S4

Orca Book Publishers
PO Box 468
Custer, WA USA
98240-0468

www.orcabook.com
Printed and bound in Canada.
Printed on 100% PCW paper.

10 09 08 07 • 4 3 2 1

For Jordann
and also for Mum and Trish

Acknowledgments

Both financial and emotional support are necessary to take a book from idea to publication. I have my families, by blood and by marriage, to thank for helping to provide me with both.

I also need to thank the Toronto Arts Council for its support, and Lusiana Lukman for bringing the grant to my attention and believing in my writing. Special thanks to my mother-in-law, Bunny, for getting me to the grant office in the nick of time.

I'd also like to thank the Self-Employment Benefits Program and all of its instructors for their support, advice and guidance.

Thank you to everyone at Orca Book Publishers, especially my editor, Sarah Harvey, for her patience and dedication. Thank you also to my agents, David and Lynn Bennett, for taking me on and for their advice and encouragement.

And finally, to my friends, who have always believed in me. Thank you.

To see a world in a grain of sand

And a heaven in a wild flower,

Hold infinity in the palm of your hand

And eternity in an hour.

—William Blake
Auguries of Innocence

Chapter One

My past is misery; my present, agony; my future, bleak. And it is *not* just because I'm a thirteen-year-old girl, or because I'm too thin or too tall, or because my hair is red (it's orange, actually—but *they* call it red).

I admit, in the big picture my life wouldn't rank very high on the downtrodden scale. Not if you compare me to a kid dying of AIDS in Africa or fearing bombs in a war zone, but who thinks about the big picture? You think about your family and friends, your school, your work, your neighbors—how you measure up.

My circle hasn't just shrunk; it's gone pear-shaped as well. In recent months it's consisted of home, school and the hospital—that's it. All of it.

Other kids' lives are a heck of a lot bigger than mine, which is ironic, considering how much smaller their minds are. Do I sound bitter? I don't mean to. I'm not bitter, I'm downright furious.

The sky sympathizes. It's an empty gray, and thunder gives voice to my fury, saving me the trouble of screaming, which I have every right to do. Especially since, on top of everything else, Dad is making me ride in the same car as The Wicked Witch of all compass points associated with anything demonic. She's pure evil in a black business suit. Her jet-black hair is tied back in a bun so tight you'd think she was trying to give herself a face-lift. Her eyes—two lumps of blackest coal—are set off by ghostly white, almost transparent, skin. Her suit does little to contain her breasts, which stick out like the noses on a pair of bloodhounds who have just caught their prey's scent—my dad being the prey. Of course he doesn't see her that way.

"It'll be okay," she stupidly says to him.

Dad *nods*.

My eyes bore hateful thoughts through the Explorer's headrest and into The Thing's brain as she sits comfortably in the passenger seat. Maybe I'll give her an aneurysm, or I'll give myself one; either would improve the situation.

The way It ogles my father makes me glad I skipped breakfast.

The sun's coming out now, shining through the trees as the rain continues to fall. The sun tries to cheer me up, outlining every dancing drop. The wind holds the beads of water in the air, giving them life. The sun-shower becomes a million tiny water babies sent to entertain me.

Late June greenery emerges emerald from the mist as we wind through the Don Valley. The rain totally disappears as Mother Sun takes her little droplets home—what was comforting suddenly seems cruel.

As we turn onto Bloor Street, I'm happy to say good-bye to the trees and wrap myself in cold steel and hardened concrete. If only I could stop the sun from keeping an eye on me. I don't feel like being sunny today.

They say life goes on. That the sun is still going to come up in the morning.

But why? Why must the sun always come up in the morning? Why can't it take a day off? Why can't we all take a day off to reflect on how screwed up everything is?

The only way to be free is to not need anything from anyone, even the sun. That way no one can hurt you or leave you when you need them the most. That's when they always go. That's when she left—when I needed her the most. What kind of a mother leaves her thirteen-year-old daughter?

This morning—the day of her funeral—I got my first period! It's like she planned it that way. Her voice comes from behind a cloud, or wherever the hell she is—pun intended. "You're a woman now and you'll have to look after yourself."

It was disgusting!

I used bunched-up toilet paper for the first two hours until Dad could "pull himself together" enough to get out of the bathroom so I could see if Mom had left any tampons; she had—thank God.

I don't know why Dad's upset. He's already found The She-devil—Mom's instant replacement. Mom and Dad were high school sweethearts from grade nine on—how do you replace that? And almost overnight!

He says The She-devil's "a friend who only wants to help us through a difficult time."

He's either naïve, stupid or lying—my money's on all three. No way am I going to let her "help" me.

"J," Billy whines, tugging my sleeve and looking up at me with urgency in his clear blue eyes. Almost everybody calls me J. Jenevieve is too long, Jen is too short and Jenny is too perky. Billy's my five-year-old brother. He's all right, in his little pinstriped suit with his blond hair cut and styled like a junior executive: straight across the back and every hair arranged perfectly on top—a mini-Dad, poor kid. Of course, Dad's hair is no longer thick enough to be perfect on top, and each year it gets closer to gray than blond. Mom wouldn't have approved of The Witch's new look for Billy.

Billy doesn't really understand what's going on—about Mom, I mean. He cried a lot at the hospital after Mom died, but I think that was just because everyone else was crying. He's been fine ever since. I'm sure he likes the fact that nobody hassles him about how much time he's spending watching TV or playing his Game Boy. He even gets to watch martial arts films on the big-screen TV instead of sneaking into my bedroom to see them. Not that *I* watch them, of course—well, only with Billy. Mom thought they were too violent, so we kept it on the down-low, sneaking them out of Dad's DVD library.

"What?" I ask, leaving out the *is it now* part of the sentence.

"I need to pee," Billy says.

"You'll have to wait till we get to the funeral home."

"I don't know if I can," he whines.

"You're going to have to," I tell him as he squeezes his crotch for dramatic effect. I can't help but feel a little sorry

for him. "We're almost there. Just think of something else."
The last thing I need today is a little brother in wet pants.

"If you could read my mind love…" I begin singing a
Gordon Lightfoot song—not the coolest, I know. Not that I
care. Mom used to sing it to get Billy to go to sleep.

We were going to see Gordon Lightfoot in concert, Mom
and me, but then she got sick. Dad said I was too young to
go on my own, and he couldn't take me because he had to
stay with Mom. He said I could go if I went with another
kid from school. Like that was going to happen—I keep my
musical tastes to myself to avoid total humiliation. Dad used
Mom's illness to get out of pretty much everything—mainly
raising Billy and me.

The Shrew glares at me in the rearview mirror as if my
singing is inappropriate. What would she know? I doubt she
has a mother; she was probably hatched from demon-seed.

Friend of the family along to help out, my butt! She's no
friend of mine. I wonder if they have holy water at funeral
homes. I could just throw some on her and be done with it.

As the car pulls to a stop, she puts her front hoof on Dad's
shoulder. Dad takes a deep breath, trying to get into character as the grieving husband.

"I'm here for you," The Creature says, oh so sympa-
thetically.

Dad opens the door, making a rapid exit as The Thing
turns to Billy and me.

"Come on, children," It instructs as if we're both five years
old. She couldn't get more patronizing.

I take Billy's hand and we're quickly out of the car. I'm
praying we make it to the washroom in time.

"That's all right, Jenevieve. I'll take your brother." I stand corrected; she can get more patronizing.

"He's fine with me," I firmly inform her.

"Jenevieve, your father doesn't need you being difficult."

She tears Billy from my side, lifts him up and cradles him on her hip.

I start to protest but catch myself just in time. I give an obedient and understanding smile and lean in to Billy.

"I'll meet you inside, okay, buddy?" I say, stroking his hair and giving him a little tickle under his arm. It does the trick.

That may not be holy water running down The Creature's side, but it'll do for now.

Chapter Two

The funeral home's chapel looks like a theater set, and I'm here to perform a bit part in Mom's final act. The audience is filled with semi-familiar faces that watch my every move with expressions that make me feel like I'm naked on stage and have forgotten all my lines. They're trying to express pity, but it turns to awkwardness and then stupidity as they approach.

"You probably don't remember me, do you?" asks a geriatric stranger who bears an eerie resemblance to an apple doll I made in grade five. "I think you were being toilet trained the last time I saw you."

Well, then I had more pressing things on my mind than remembering you, didn't I?

"I used to change your diapers."

Oh yes, now I remember. You were the one who brought the especially soft wipes.

"How are you?"

"How are you doing?"

"How are you holding up?"

These questions are all very popular at Mom's funeral. "How are you holding up?" is my personal favorite; at least it acknowledges that something has knocked me down.

But—"How are you?"

Great, just great! Oh, did I mention my mom just died? Think about it!

Then there's the classic—"That's too bad."

It's too bad when you miss an episode of your favorite show or when the corner store's out of the candy you like. It's catastrophic when your mom dies. I mean, come on. What's next? "Bad luck. Have you thought about getting a cat?"

How these people remember to breathe is beyond me. The fact that I actually share the same genes with some of them disturbs me to no end. Thank God I only see them at weddings and funerals, which are pretty much the same thing.

The only difference I can see is that at weddings everyone pretends to be happy when really they're miserable because they wish it was them standing at the front of the chapel. At funerals everyone pretends to be sad when they're actually happy that it's not them lying at the front of the chapel.

Besides that, I don't see much of a difference—except maybe for the dancing and the clothes, although for most guys it's only the ties that change. The faces are the same; everyone sits quietly through a boring service, and then there's a reception where everyone eats, gets drunk and talks crap.

I'm not going to drink when I get older. I don't see what the attraction is in consuming something that will make you even dumber than you already are. People, you're stupid enough. *Trust me.* Oh, wonderful. Great-aunt Milly. The woman has an entire beard growing out of one ginormous mole stuck squarely in the center of her chin. You'd think that it would only appear at a full moon, but the thing seems to be there all the time, night or day, rain or shine. God, even I know about waxing.

Aunt Milly descends with her arms stretched out, ready to engulf me in a smothering embrace.

"J," Dad's voice cracks as he gently grabs my arm, rescuing me from a fate worse than…well, from a horrible fate anyway. I'd be grateful, if I hadn't guessed what was coming.

I look to the back of the funeral home and see The Evil One—who disappeared during the reception line—has returned in an expensive new outfit. She's holding Billy's hand. He's wearing a new pair of khakis and a god-awful black sweater with white lilies on it. He looks like one of the floral arrangements that surround the coffin.

The Witch insisted on going to the department store down the street for new clothes. Apparently she spent half an hour picking out a fresh suit for herself, and then she grabbed Billy's clothes from the sale rack in the Little Miss section on the way out the door.

Dad squeezes my arm; it's time.

We slowly make our way to the front. There's an open casket. *They* say it's better that way, that it gives you a chance to say good-bye. All these chances to say good-bye. Just go already.

I hate this; it's the longest walk ever. They're not going to let Billy go up. *They* say he's too young. *I* say, if he's not too young to lose his mother, he's not too young to see her dead.

If there *is* anything to this whole open casket thing, then Billy should get his chance too, don't you think? And if there *isn't*, then what am I doing here?

The closer I get, the more surreal it feels. The light reflects off Mom's forehead, making her look like wax. Blush turns her gray cheeks pink; lipstick turns her brown lips red. She looks better than she has in months. This death thing has done her a world of good.

I feel Dad's hand tighten on mine as we take our places beside the coffin. He's quivering. I'm not quivering, and I'm not feeling the way I should; at least I don't think I am. But then again, this is my first mother-dying experience, so I'm not really sure what I should be feeling.

She's so beautiful. I hope I look that good at my funeral. Heck, I hope I look that good at my wedding, not that I'm thinking of getting married any time soon—or any time at all.

Oh God, Dad's quiver is turning into a shake. He's going to lose it. Please don't let him lose it, please. The casket, look at the casket, so nice and shiny. The grain in the wood flows like waves, like waves of energy frozen in time, trapped, trapped in this box, longing to flow again, to move again.

Wake up, damn it, wake up! All these people have come to see you! They're here for you and you're just lying there! You would never have let me get away with this, never.

My cheeks; my cheeks are wet. How did they get to be wet? I look up and see Dad crying. Could some of his tears have landed on my cheeks?

I feel him pull away.

Oh my god! It's The Creature! He's gone into the arms of Satan right in front of my mother's coffin! How inappropriate is that?

Hello, distraught daughter over here! This is unbelievable. I turn to see the crowd's reaction, but they don't even notice as The Predator drags her prey away from me.

I see Billy in the back, being mauled by Aunt Milly. He looks toward me for rescue. I get down on one knee and extend my arms. He obligingly runs into them—it's his turn to say good-bye.

I pick Billy up so that he can see our mother.

"Mom," he says.

"She's gone, Billy," I reply.

"No, she's not. She's sleeping."

"But she's never going to wake up."

"Why?"

"Because she's too tired. The sickness took all her energy away," I explain.

I feel Billy being pulled from my arms by The Beast. It must have already devoured its first victim and be hungry for more.

"Just what do you think you're doing?" The Thing snarls.

"Letting him say good-bye," I calmly reply.

"I want to see my mom!" Billy demands as he struggles to get away from The Witch's clutches, his head over her shoulder. He can't see the body.

The body. I hate saying that.

"He's too young," It states.

"*He* has a right. More right than *you*—that's for sure."

"Your dad doesn't need this today, *young lady*," The Thing says in a harsh whisper so no one else can hear. With the help of Billy's cries, she's successful.

"Let him see her," I insist, reaching for Billy.

She turns so that he's just out of my grasp. Then, while holding Billy with one arm, she grabs me with the other. I look over to Dad. He's being babied by Great-aunt Milly and can't see the peril his children are in—nobody can.

The Witch has shrouded us with some sort of invisibility spell, probably created by the bat's breath that she releases from her mouth.

"That's enough!" It says. "You're impossible. Your mother is well rid of you!" She releases my arm and immediately puts on a fake smile before slithering back to Dad. Visible again, The Creature casts a wave of silence behind her that begins to smother me as I stand alone with my mother's mannequin.

The hush entombs every crack and crevice of this empty room filled with empty minds and an empty body. It gets louder and louder, the quiet crushing me till I can bear the weight no longer. My mouth opens and a shattering scream forces out every inch of the calm that had no place there to begin with—my mother always hated quiet.

After emptying my lungs, I look around the room and realize that my scream has transformed the spell of silence into one of immobility. Everyone stands like statues, staring at me with balloon eyes.

Fortunately the paralyzing spell doesn't have any hold on me. I refill my powerful lungs with enough air to carry me as fast and as far as I can go.

Chapter Three

Sitting on the grass in the middle of High Park, blocks away from the funeral home, head between my knees, I watch ants carry things into their farm, and I try to forget that I just ran away from my own mother's funeral.

Why is it called an ant farm? Shouldn't it really be called an ant *site*? Ants are more like construction workers than farmers. Their exoskeletons are like hard hats, covering them so their little bodies won't get hurt as they work.

"I suppose it should be," says a gentle female voice. I look up at the most beautiful woman I've ever seen—she looks very familiar, but I can't think why.

She's in her thirties or forties, it's hard to tell which. Her hair is long and untamed, and she's wearing a flowing burgundy sundress that floats under a well-worn jean jacket. Her belt and matching earrings look very aboriginal—linked silver discs with a sun design and an all-seeing turquoise eye in the center. Her necklace is a circle of silver dolphins leaping around another turquoise stone. Too New Age hippie to be cool, but at least it's not a business suit, so score one for the stranger.

"What?" I ask as my hand touches my cheek, which feels as though I've just been swimming. I turn away and try to dry it with my sleeve before she notices. More pity I don't need.

The stranger kneels down beside me.

"It should be called a site," she says.

"How did you know what I was thinking?"

She continues to look at the ground. A small smile moves across her face.

"Oh, crap. I was talking to myself, wasn't I?" I say. "I'm not crazy. I just do that once in a while. Talk to myself, I mean, but I never answer—myself. I mean, I know it's me talking. I just don't always know when it's out loud."

She looks at me with understanding eyes. "It's okay. I do that quite often too. I find that one can have some very interesting conversations without the interruptions of others. Wouldn't you agree?"

She reaches out and touches my shoulder. She seems harmless enough, but I don't like this sign of familiarity, no matter how kind she sounds or how familiar she looks. I jump up and move away from her.

"What are you doing?" I ask.

"You seemed in need of a hug," she replies.

"Well, I'm not," I say.

"My mistake," she apologizes.

"Are you a pedophile? 'Cause I know all about pedophiles, so don't try anything."

She laughs, but it doesn't seem to be at me.

"You don't mince words, do you?" she says.

"I may be young, but I don't see that as an excuse to waste time."

"You're very wise for your age."

"Sorry, perhaps I missed it. Who are you?"

"Straight to the point. I like that. I'm your Aunt Guinevere, Jenevieve."

"Okay, I don't know how you know my name, but I don't have an Aunt Guinevere. The only aunt I have is Dad's Aunt Milly, and she's as dense as my dad. It seems to run in that side of the family. I'm hoping to avoid it."

"Your father has a good heart. He may not always have the courage to do anything with it, but he does have a good heart."

"Whatever," I say. "That still doesn't tell me who you are."

"I'm your mother's big sister."

"My mother doesn't have any sisters—or didn't."

"Now that's not a very bright thing for such an intelligent girl to say. If she doesn't have any sisters, then who am I?"

"That's what I want to know."

"But I've told you."

"And I told you that my mother didn't have any sisters."

"You see, this is why I prefer talking to myself—fewer disagreements."

What is she talking about?

"Do you not believe your own eyes?" she continues.

"I do, and they're telling me that I've never seen you before."

"Your mind has more than memory, so look closer and listen harder."

She stretches her hand out and places it next to mine. Hers is older and slightly larger, yet our hands are somehow the same. Examining her hair more closely, I see how it matches mine. Lighter, more beautiful, but again the same. The longer I look at her face, the more she looks like... Mom.

"Now," she asks, "can you see?"

Before I know it, my cheeks are getting wet again. I quickly get *that* under control.

"Where did you come from?" I ask, looking around. "How did you find me? Why haven't I met you before?"

"Questions, questions. And we'll have time to answer them all, but first we'd better get you back to the funeral home."

"I'd really rather not."

"I'd rather not too," she says, leaving out the *but we have to* part of the sentence.

She stands up and extends her hand to me. I know I'm going to have to return sooner or later, and it would be better to do so with an ally. At least, I hope that's what she is.

Chapter Four

Walking back to the funeral home is terrifying. The knot in my stomach makes its way up to the base of my throat and I feel sick.

On the doorstep, my feet decide to grow roots, ripping through the concrete to embed themselves in the ground. My legs become a solid trunk, and I pray that the rest of me will transform into an ornamental tree so that I can stand out here forever and be admired rather than enter the chapel and be despised.

Aunt Guinevere grabs my hand and gives it a reassuring squeeze. Her eyes throw a protective shield around me. A few tears trickle down my cheek and fall to the ground. Their salt kills the roots and allows me to move forward. The sickness temporarily subsides.

We re-enter the funeral home. It's as if I never left. The room is still frozen. All eyes, once again, are on me.

The Witch's glare locks onto me. She swoops like an owl on a mouse, but before she can get her talons around me, Dad grabs her arm.

He isn't looking at her, or at me, but at Aunt Guinevere. I look up at Aunt Guinevere, who's looking at Dad intently yet tenderly. Aunt Guinevere nods. Dad turns and whispers something to The Creature. She says something back in an obviously disagreeable manner. Dad ignores her.

His eyes turn to me as he leaves The She-devil's side with such a determined step that it makes me feel I should get out of the way. The Evil One watches him, hands on her hips, a *Well, I never* expression on her face. She tightens her grip on Billy's hand, causing him to wince and, using his whole body, pull free.

Dad grabs me and gives me a big hug, the biggest since the hospital, which was the biggest he'd ever given me. He's not really a hugging guy, or he wasn't. Now he holds me so tight that I think I'm going to pop.

Girl crushed to death by father at mother's funeral.

As if the other kids don't think I'm a big-enough freak as it is, but to die like that—I wouldn't be able to show my face at my own funeral.

"We have to say good-bye now," he says in a tender voice, like I had done nothing wrong.

Dad takes hold of my hand and we walk back over to The She-demon. Then something *amazing* happens: Dad doesn't look at her. He extends his hand to Billy, who takes it.

"What are you doing?" The Serpent hisses.

Dad doesn't reply.

The three of us—me, Dad and Billy—walk up to the casket. It feels like years pass in this once-again silent room. But the silence is different this time—it's comforting.

As we arrive at the coffin, everyone else in the room disappears. It's just the four of us now, a proper family again.

I don't want to be here, but I also don't want to leave this place where nothing is real and it's all too real to bear. My body tingles with numbness. I want this play to end and Mom to take her bow so we can all go home.

Dad releases my hand and I turn quickly, expecting to see The Hunter returning for its prey, but Dad has only let go in order to lift Billy. When Billy is secure in Dad's arms, Dad grabs my hand again.

He squeezes my hand while putting his head against Billy's head. Billy looks so lost as the tears start to well in Dad's eyes, but it's not the sobbing it was before. This time Dad's doing his best to hold it together.

"Never forget how much she loves you," he chokes out as he gives my hand another squeeze to make sure I understand that the sentiment is also meant for me.

Instinctively I answer with a hand squeeze of my own. All the tingles swarm together to form a ball in the base of my throat, choking me and causing my eyes to water. I'm not sure who this man is, but for these frozen moments, he seems like a father.

Billy stares blankly at Mom and then, with a wiggle, silently asks Dad to put him down. When Dad does, Billy comes around and grabs my free hand. He stares at the floor, rocking impatiently.

I guess he's said his good-byes, or maybe he's decided

that the body in the casket isn't really Mom, so he can't say good-bye. Perhaps he doesn't understand this is good-bye, or he knows it isn't. I wish I knew. Oh, how I wish I knew.

Dad, free from Billy, reaches over and sets his hand on Mom's forehead. He leans in and kisses her gently.

"I love you," he whispers, and then he straightens up, puts his shoulders back in an unnaturally rigid stance and swallows deeply.

"Come on," he says.

The man from the funeral home is in front of us as we turn.

"Right this way," he instructs, ushering us out of the chapel toward a side room. As we leave, I turn and look over my shoulder to see what he is moving us away from. A man and a woman from the funeral home are preparing to close the casket. I turn away before they actually do the deed. Watching would make it too final.

Chapter Five

Before we even get to the door of the small side room—I want to call it a waiting room, but the idea of a waiting room at a funeral parlor is just too creepy—The Thing swoops in and snatches Dad away.

He releases my hand and I stop dead in the aisle—if you'll pardon the expression—feeling a banshee scream forming deep within, but before it can dislodge the lump from my throat, a hand softly grips my shoulder. I look up at Aunt Guinevere, whose eyes offer support as her touch calms me.

After we enter the side room, the undertaker closes the door to give us some time to ourselves while they finish with the casket.

There's a large leather couch and two matching chairs, but we all stand in the center with our heads down, like we're in some sort of prayer circle. I start to feel claustrophobic.

I look to Aunt Guinevere for comfort and find myself wondering why no one else seems to notice her and why Dad hasn't said anything to her. And then it dawns on me— she isn't real.

I've lost my mind! My brilliant mind. The stress has taken me over the edge and I'm starting to see people who aren't even there. Oh, this isn't good; this is so far from good—even if the imaginary person is brighter than the real people.

Okay, don't look at her, don't talk to her, don't let anyone know that you're seeing things. But I *feel* her hand on my shoulder. Can you *feel* a hallucination? Well, that's a dumb question. I *feel* her.

I keep my head down and try to act sane. Fortunately, considering the circumstances and the company, I have a lot of leeway.

"How are you, Gerald?" my hallucination asks Dad.

"Guinevere?" Dad sees my hallucination too. Oh my god. We're both going mad and he seems relieved about it. "When I saw you I thought…it's been a long time."

"Who's this, Gerald?" asks The Wicked One.

Wait a minute. If they can both see her—oh praise be!— I'm not nuts! Not as nuts as originally suspected, anyway.

"Fanny," Dad says, calling The Beast by name, "this is Anastasia's sister, Guinevere."

"Pleased to meet you," The Beast says with all the sincerity of a scorpion on a frog's back, promising not to sting. She extends her stinger, which Aunt Guinevere graciously shakes while staring directly into her eyes.

My eyes travel back and forth between them like I'm watching a tennis match with a neck brace on. Fanny serves a hard and fast dirty look, showing Aunt Guinevere on whose court she's playing. Aunt Guinevere boldly meets the glare, returning it with such confident ease that it throws her opponent off. Shaken, but not fallen, Fanny sizes up Guinevere's wardrobe with a quick once-over, and then she lobs up stern disapproval. Guinevere follows with a warm and gentle smile that says, *That's the best you've got? Doesn't even warrant a mention.* Fanny's been put completely off her game. Unable to even attempt a return, she smiles nervously, nods, turns and stalks off the court. Before crossing the foul line, The Wicked Creature is restored to her evil self and throws a menacing look over her shoulder, letting her adversary know there'll be a rematch.

Guinevere spots Billy, who is still a growth on the end of my arm.

"And you must be Billy. I'm your Aunt Guinevere," she says, extending her hand.

Billy attaches himself to my hip.

"Mom's dead," he blurts out.

"Only in the most basic sense," Aunt Guinevere tells him.

"I'm never going to see her again," Billy says. "They told me so."

"They did, did they?" Aunt Guinevere replies. "Close your eyes."

Billy's eyes get wider when she says this.

"Go on, close them," she tells him, waving her hand gently over Billy's face without touching it.

Billy nods and closes his eyes.

"Think about your mom," she says. "Do you see her?"

"Yeah."

"What's she doing?"

"She's smiling at me."

"And I'll bet if you try you can hear her too."

"Yeah."

Fanny watches in disapproval.

"What's she saying?"

"No cookies before dinner."

Aunt Guinevere's smile widens as she holds back a laugh.

"There you have it then," she says. "I guess they don't know sh—!"

"That's completely inappropriate, " Fanny says, doing her best to drown out the forbidden word, the sound of which causes Billy's eyes to pop open. And I must admit mine get a little larger too.

But as Billy's giggle rises for the first time in over a week, I see that it was more than appropriate—it was necessary.

"We're ready for you now," says the undertaker, who has entered the room unnoticed.

I don't think anyone's ready for Aunt Guinevere.

The Evil One darts in to grab my dad's hand. I can't even begin to list how many things are wrong with that little maneuver. I feel my blood start to boil—as Aunt Milly would say—then a cool hand touches my head. I look up at Aunt Guinevere, who's extending her other hand to Billy while turning her back on Dad and Fanny.

I force a halfsmile, trying to wipe away my anger. I remember Sunday school and turning the other cheek, but I can't help but think that if Jesus met Fanny, his advice would change.

Chapter Six

The undertaker leads us back to the chapel and steps aside to let us pass. I half expect him to announce us, like we're the royal family arriving at a party. This is so unbelievably messed up.

The coffin is closed. Mom's hidden away from everything now. Maybe that's why she left us—she couldn't take it anymore; she couldn't take *us* anymore. She just wanted to get away. My whining, my constant bitching. I complained about having to go to the hospital, and I threw a tantrum so I could go to a school dance—a *stupid* school dance.

I didn't even want to go to the dance. I just didn't want to be told I couldn't. I was sick of her getting all the attention all the time. Maybe she *is* well rid of me, better off in that box than with us. She must have thought so or she never would have let it happen.

The minister drones on about God and Jesus and the love of our Lord and how it's all-forgiving. If God's love is all-forgiving, then why do I feel like I'm being punished? And the part about how he loves us all equally? Why does he make some of our lives so much harder than others? Why do I lose my mother while those other girls—the little clueless wonders He apparently loves equally—still have theirs and will most likely continue to have them when they start dating, have their first kiss, graduate, get married, have kids. Whatever they do, they'll have their moms. If you believe what the minister is saying, mine will be forever with Jesus. What does Jesus need her for? He's got millions of followers; I have no one!

I start to hum to try and tune it out, which draws some pretty nasty looks from a lot of people—not just Satan in her second black suit. Are you even supposed to wear black if you're not related? What is the protocol? Not that The Vulture would care. I wouldn't be surprised if, before she found Dad, she used to circle other women's funerals, looking for lonely widowers.

Aunt Guinevere isn't wearing black, and she's also not giving me dirty looks. She doesn't even notice that I'm humming. She seems to be in her own little world, her expression neither happy nor sad.

I stop humming and start looking over the crowd. I see some of the girls from school—girls I used to be friends with. Their mothers probably dragged them here.

I listen to the minister go on and on about how horrible it is to see a mother taken away from her children.

"Take comfort in the time you had together," he instructs

us, "and know that she is watching over you and will be there to guide you wherever life's path takes you. And remember that she will go on living in you and in the memories you have of her."

Why do people keep saying that? A memory can't hug you. It can't stroke your hair when you're feeling sick or cheer for you at a school concert or make you a birthday cake.

"So you can stick the memories up your robe."

Now, that last bit wasn't supposed to be out loud. But judging by everyone's face, I may've done my thinking a little louder than I meant to.

I look up at Aunt Guinevere and grab her hand. She looks down at me and smiles, then looks off again. After what seems like hours, the minister continues his sermon. I lean against Aunt Guinevere, avoiding eye contact with everyone and using all my brainpower not to think.

Chapter Seven

The graveside service is mercifully short. Dad keeps his weeping under control. As I place the rose on the coffin, I feel nauseated. I put my hand into the pile of fresh earth, the world spins out of control. I barely hit the grave when I toss the dirt.

The only thing that keeps me from throwing up is Billy, who stares at me for answers. He doesn't want to be here. He doesn't understand why he has to be and he wants me to explain. Of course I can't. The best that I can do is not add to his confusion by projectile vomiting onto the casket. Mind you, he might find it funny.

I see Aunt Guinevere standing back from the grave. Her expression hasn't really changed, but there is a trace of sadness in it now. A forced smile pushes a tear out of the corner of one of her eyes. I smile back.

After the ceremony we go back to our house, which

quickly fills with people. Everyone seems to have turned out for the reception.

I stand in the kitchen doorway. The nausea hasn't left and I feel like I haven't slept in years. I eat a few little pickles and some tiny sandwiches, hoping food will help. It doesn't.

"I'm going to go up to bed," I say to Dad at the first opportunity.

"Fine," he says, not bothering to look at me.

I go to say good-bye to Aunt Guinevere, who's on the couch watching a martial arts movie with Billy. It's one I've seen so often that I could probably do all the moves, but I still can't remember the name—*Dragon something* or *something Dragon*.

I watch as the main character uses his foot to flick a pole off the ground in front of him. He takes his enemy down with a quick hit to the groin and a strike under the chin. Then he pirouettes—in much the same way I used to in ballet class—and drives the butt end of the pole into another guy's chest, sending him flying. Getting into his crouching tiger stance and tucking the end of the pole under his armpit, he says—in a horribly obvious dubbed-in voice—"You are not ready for the fight you have started. Leave now or meet a most painful demise."

And his enemies run off. How unrealistic is that!

"Night, Aunt Guin," I say. "Is it all right if I call you Aunt Guin?"

"You can call me Aunt Dibilybop if you like," she replies. "Why are you saying goodnight in the afternoon?"

"I'm not feeling well. Why would I call you Aunt Dibilybop?"

"You might like the sound of it," she replies. "If you're not feeling well tomorrow, I'll mix something up for you."

"Are you staying here?" I inquire.

"Can I call you Aunt Dibilybop?" Billy interrupts.

"Of course you can," she says, giving him a sideways hug. "I'm not staying here, but I'll be back again tomorrow, if you like."

"I would," I tell her.

"So would I," she says, never taking her eyes off the television.

Once in bed, I pull as many blankets around me as I can find. I don't care how hot it makes me; I want it to feel like someone is holding me. Closing my eyes, I quickly drift into the cold comfort of sleep, hoping to find Mom.

Chapter Eight

There's one precious fleeting moment in each day when everything is all right again. It happens in the morning, although perhaps it's the night that should be given the credit for conjuring up the bittersweet images that come to comfort me.

In that single moment—the one that lies between waking and dreaming—my spirit can go beyond where my body chains me; between light and darkness, fantasy and reality, how things are and how they should be. In this place, she is waiting.

Before the funeral, the hospital, the illness, the gray skin; before the fearful mornings, hoping she had made it through the night; before the guilt from wanting it to be over; before the helplessness of watching as she became weaker and weaker; before Dad got more and more distant; before the doctors; before the diagnosis and, most importantly, before

the sadness—the eternal sadness and the relentless anger—
she comes into my room, wakes me with a gentle touch,
caressing the side of my face as she moves the hair back
and tucks it behind my ear so she can give me a kiss on the
cheek.

She used to do that all the time. Sometimes I'd pretend
to be sleeping until she did. I never told her that. I told her I
was too old for such things and that I wished she'd stop.

"No one is ever too old for their mother's love," she
would say, giving me a hug, tickling my ribs and telling me
to get up.

In that place, the place between this world and the next,
I can feel her caring touch, the love in her kiss and sometimes, if I get to stay long enough (which I rarely do), the
safety of her arms around me.

My time with her this morning is cut short by the sound
of a pounding hoof. Someone must have taught The Beast
how to count to ten and she's practicing on my door. She
does it twice. The first time she only makes it to eight, gets
confused and has to start again.

"What?" I yell at the end of her second set. She makes it
all the way to ten this time—perhaps there's hope.

"There's no need to scream," she bellows, barging into
my room.

"*What* does not mean *enter*." I figure since she's doing so
well with math, we'll move on to English.

She sighs loudly, shaking her head at me. I may have
confused her—too much information, too fast. She starts
picking my clothes up off the floor.

"What are you doing?" I ask politely.

"Your behavior yesterday was inappropriate, to say the least," she says.

"Why are you touching my clothes?" I ask, to clarify.

"I don't think you even know what appropriate behavior is. You don't even know how to clean up after yourself," she sneers.

"Put my clothes down, please," I calmly request.

"You ruined the day," she says.

My calmness abandons me.

"You can't ruin something that can't get any worse, you insensitive—" I hate it when my brain goes blank at the most inappropriate time—"cow!" Not very creative, I admit—and for all I know, cows may be very sensitive. Perhaps that's why they're vegetarians. Nonetheless, from the look on her face, I've hit my mark.

She throws the clothes down.

"I'm sorry that you find me so difficult to tolerate. But don't worry. It won't be for much longer," she says as she turns and storms out.

The nausea erupts and I rush into my bathroom, where all the little pickles and sandwiches from the reception are released into the bowl.

I should have chewed more, I think, staring at the baby gherkins floating on top. The egg salad and cold cuts don't make a pretty combination, so I flush and watch the little pickles spin faster and faster until they disappear.

They get going so fast at the end that I'm afraid they might take off out of the bowl and go flying around the room or, worse yet, the house. That'd be a hard one to explain. I should have fished one out and slipped it onto the side of

Fanny's plate. That would have been fun, especially when she ate it—yummy.

"Wait a minute," I say to myself. "It won't be for much longer? What did she mean by that?"

I quickly rinse my mouth out, throw on some clothes and dash downstairs. I stop just outside the kitchen door.

"It's the best thing for her," I hear. "You'll be working too much to be able to give her the attention she needs. And when you aren't working, you have to look after yourself and Billy."

What seed is the Demon Farmer sowing?

"You're right. I know you're right," Dad says in his usual mindless tone.

"Whatcha' doin'?"

I jump at the sound of Billy's voice. He's in the hallway on the other side of the living room. For such a little guy, his voice can *really* carry. I turn and glare at him, but it's too late; I can hear the clip-clop of her hoofs fast approaching. Deciding to enter, I wait an extra second before pushing open the swinging door. *THUD.*

"Oh, I'm sorry, I didn't know you were there!" I apologize to her in my nicest voice.

The Thing cups her face as tears rise to the fire in her eyes and lava runs from her nose. Dad jumps to her rescue.

"Tilt your head forward," he instructs while pinching her nose for her—such a gentleman. "Jenevieve!" he yells.

"It was an accident," I protest, choked up at the very *thought* that I'd *purposely* do such a thing.

"Just be more careful," he says, almost apologizing.

Fanny starts to open her mouth but catches herself.

Leaving her teeth clenched, she gives me a *you'll get yours* glare. When Dad looks away, I manage a little smirk for her benefit.

Say it, Evil One. Show your horns and say it. Say what a nasty little creature you think I am. Say how I'm out to get you. Say it, say it, say it! Show Dad what you really think of me. Come on, *please*.

"It's not broken, but you should keep your head forward until the bleeding stops," he says while helping her over to a chair.

Her eyes never leave me. I take the opportunity to wink. It looks like that may have done it. Her mouth opens and lets in air for the first time since the collision. Oxygen reaches that *nasty* little brain, but instead of speaking, It smiles.

Well, it's not really a smile, not a normal-person smile anyway. More like how you would picture Satan at Armageddon. "Oh, I'm okay," It finally says. "Accidents do happen. Why don't we share our plans with J?"

I hate it when *she* calls me J.

"J, have a seat," Dad says in a worried voice. He sits oh-so-slowly and avoids eye contact.

"I'm okay," I tell him.

It will require so much less effort to storm out if I remain standing.

"Please," he says, still avoiding eye contact.

"No, really." The faster I can get out of here the better.

He lifts his head. His eyes, that look. I've seen it before, but not on him.

We had this dog once, a chocolate Lab named Spiral. He was Mom's dog and he was part of the family before I was.

I loved that dog. When Spiral got old, he had problems controlling his bodily functions. Sometimes he would lose control of them on the way to the door, leaving little sticky chocolate arrows from the living room to the yard. Mom and Dad would have put him to sleep if they could have figured out a way to do it without traumatizing me.

Eventually Spiral did die, and I had a meltdown for a night and depression for a week, but at least I knew we hadn't killed him, which, in hindsight, we probably should have done. I was just too young and selfish to realize that keeping something alive while it's in pain isn't love, it's fear. I've thought about that a lot in the last few months—too much.

Anyway, Spiral used to get this look on his face directly following these little accidents. Not embarrassed. More like *I have no control over this. I know it's crap but it is what it is; please accept me for who I am or put me out of my misery.*

That's what Dad has become—an animal who's lost control of himself. Since scratching behind his ears and telling him *It's okay, boy, we still love you* isn't an option, I take a seat.

"We've been…," he starts.

"*We?*" I say.

He looks up at me, sees where I'm going and changes his approach.

"*I've* been thinking it over. I know this is a tough time for you—for all of us—and I don't think I'm going to be able to give you the attention you need. I have to get back to my practice."

"I'm sure your patients will understand if you take some time off," I say.

"I've taken a lot of time off and they've been incredibly understanding, that's why I need…"

"You need?"

"I have a responsibility."

"Yes, you do."

"When you're older you'll understand," he says.

"Why work is more important than family? I hope I never understand that."

Dad can't even look at me now, and his helplessness causes his face to morph completely into Spiral's. I lean slightly to the side and check under his chair for a fresh chocolate roll.

"You're going to camp for the summer," he says.

"What?"

"It's for the best," he tells me, still looking down.

"For who?" I ask, looking at The Evil Puppeteer as a smile appears under her bloody nose.

Dad still won't look at me.

"What, is there some kind of special mourning camp set up for loser kids who've lost a parent? Oh, that'll cheer me up just fine. The dances alone must be so much fun. Does it come with Kleenex included? Or should I bring my own? What am I thinking? They're probably the sponsors— *Welcome to Camp Two-ply with Aloe.*"

"Your attitude isn't helping anyone," Dad says.

"Actually it's making me feel loads better," I say, looking at the mastermind behind this whole plan. She's smirking. That would infuriate me further if it weren't for the crusty blood on her upper lip that brings a trickle of joy into my heart. "Nice ventriloquism, by the way," I say to her. "You don't even have to stick your hand up his…"

"That's enough!" Dad yells, finally raising his head.

It's far from enough, but it'll do for now.

"It's not a mourners' camp. It's a regular camp with some excellent counselors. Fanny knows the people who run it, and she says it's amazing."

Oh my god, there'll be classes in cat sacrificing!

"I'm not going!" I state.

"Jenevieve!" Dad says, leaving out the *it's not up for discussion* part of the sentence.

"You know, Dad, if all you can do without Mom is leave a trail of crap everywhere you go, you could at least have your new owner follow you around with a shovel," I say, turning to Fanny. "But I suppose you'd be more comfortable with a broom."

She straightens her head to look at me, and blood flows out her nose before she remembers and tilts her head forward while tightening the pinch again.

I turn back to Dad. He looks almost as angry as I feel. I think that's fair.

"J," he says, trying to act calm, "I just can't handle…"

"Me," I say.

His slow response tells me I'm right, and as I stand up to charge out of the room, I hear a calming voice behind me.

"She's more than welcome to come and stay with me."

I look around to see Aunt Guin. I don't know how long she's been there, but the tension in the room doesn't seem to affect her in the slightest. She enters with grace and a smile. She comes directly to me and kisses me on the top of my head.

"Billy let me in. I hope you don't mind." She looks over at Fanny, who has straightened her head, letting the red river run again. Aunt Guin points to her own upper lip to remind Fanny about her nose. After a few seconds, Fanny realizes what Aunt Guin is referring to and tilts her head forward. Gerbils learn faster, they really do.

"No, of course not," my dad says.

He seems more relaxed when Aunt Guin is around too. In fact, the only one who doesn't is Fanny, which makes me like Aunt Guin even more.

"I'll go with Aunt Guin. That'd be okay with me."

"It's not up to you," Dad replies.

"No, why should it be? It's only *my* life."

Dad shakes his head and lowers it with a *you're too young to understand* sigh.

I hate it when he patronizes me. Aunt Guin puts her hand on my shoulder. Oh God, not her too. But her expression is not patronizing at all. It says *leave it to me.*

"Guinevere, I couldn't ask you to…," Dad begins.

"I offered, so you're not asking. I just bought a place in the country, and I need help fixing it up. It could be a summer job for J. Besides, it would give us a chance to get to know each other."

Dad continues to ponder, and as he does, Fanny starts to get nervous. I can't even imagine what's in store for me at Camp Weep-we-do.

"You'd be doing me a favor," Aunt Guin says. "Well…"

"The camp has already been booked." The Devil has risen.

It must be some kind of brainwashing camp and that's

why she wants me to go there. Maybe she's booked me in for a lobotomy.

"I don't know if we can get a refund," she adds.

Dad's thinking—always a dangerous sign.

"I don't mean to be pushing my way in here." (Aunt Guin, what are you saying? Push, *push*.) "If I'm adding to your stress…" (A lesson for all, never trust an adult no matter how nice they appear.) "I have another idea." (It better be good.) "J goes to camp," (Not good, not good.) "and I'll stay right here and help out. We have a lot of years to catch up on too, Gerald." Aunt Guin reaches across the table and touches Dad's hand. "And you'll need all the support you can get at this difficult time."

"What am I thinking?" The Demon cackles. "I know the owners, so of course we can get a refund. And what could be nicer for J than a chance to get to know her aunt. Family is so important at a time like this. Oh, Gerald, you have to let her go."

"Okay," he says, sounding as confused as I feel.

"It's settled then," Aunt Guin says. "Come on, J. I'll help you pack." She turns and starts to walk out of the room.

I'm not sure what just happened, but I wish I'd paid closer attention.

Chapter Nine

As soon as we enter my room, Aunt Guin starts to go through my stuff. I suppose I should mind, but she does it like a little kid, curious about her surroundings. Most adults look over a teenager's room like a cop going over a crime scene, giving an impromptu interrogation as they look for evidence. "What's *this* about?"

"*This* one says *explicit* lyrics!"

"Where did *you* get *this*?"

"*Who* got you *that*?"

There's none of that with Aunt Guin.

"Is this your favorite?" she asks, pulling out my *Wizard of Oz* DVD.

"I guess," I tell her.

"Mine too," she says, returning it to its shelf.

"Oh, and this one's also my favorite," she says, looking at my DVD of *A Midsummer Night's Dream*.

"How can you have two favorites?" I ask.

"You can have as many favorites as you like," she tells me. "So what shall we bring on our adventure, do you think?" she says cheerfully.

"I'm thirteen. I'm getting a little too old for adventures. A trip will be fine." I want to make it clear to her that I'm much more mature than your average giggly teen. There's no need for her to act like Happy Barbie.

"Oh, how awful for you. So what should you take on your trip? That sounds so terribly boring, a trip. You're bound to end up landing on your face if you trip, and who wants that?" She talks while exploring, and it's hard to tell if she is actually talking to me or just rambling away to herself. She stops and looks at me. She must have asked me something, but I got so caught up in listening that I stopped hearing.

"What?" I ask.

"Who?"

I look around to see who she's talking about.

"Where?" I inquire.

"How?" she responds.

"How? Why…"

"Why? And that's all you need to become a journalist."

My aunt's insane. I'm spending my summer with a crazy lady. Great, just great. Mourners' camp isn't sounding quite so bad.

"So is it all right?" she asks.

"What?" I say without thinking.

"Who?" she says playfully.

"No, no, no. What I meant was…is what all right?"

"To call it a voyage instead of a trip?" she says.

"Doesn't a voyage have to be by water?" I ask.

"A voyage is an expedition, especially by water or in air or in space. And really, how far can one get without water or air, and the whole planet is in space and so are we."

Some of us more than others.

"I suppose so," I agree, too confused to do otherwise.

"So a voyage it will be then?"

"You know what?" I say. "I think an adventure would be just fine."

"Ah, an adventure! Now, that's the reckless spirit that got us over the Rockies."

"Okay then." I have no idea what she's talking about. None.

"You might want to look through the bag to see if there's anything else you'll need. Oh wait, the bathroom."

As she disappears into the bathroom, I look at my bed, where my backpack sits, already packed. I walk over and look in. My clothes are neatly folded and she has packed my favorite CDs and books. Aunt Guin comes out of the bathroom carrying my makeup bag. My expression reveals my shock.

"What's the matter? Have I overstepped the boundaries? I do that sometimes," she says sincerely.

"How did you do that?"

"Do what?"

"Pack my bag."

"Opened the bag up and put the stuff in. It wasn't that tricky, really. Have you never packed a bag before?"

What is most baffling is that there never seems to be even a hint of sarcasm in her voice.

"That's not what I mean and you know it."

"No, I really don't." She almost seems startled by my abruptness, and as I look her over, I realize that she genuinely doesn't get it.

"How did you do it without me seeing you?"

"You didn't see me pack it?"

"No."

"But you were standing there the whole time."

"And I was watching you the whole time."

"Really? Ah well, it's done now. No worries," she says and puts my makeup bag into my backpack.

"There are worries. I'm worried! Quite worried actually."

"About what?" Again, completely genuine.

"About what?" I point to the bag. She looks at it as if she's already forgotten about it.

"Are you still on about that?"

Oh, that weepy camp is looking really good now.

"My eyes never left you."

"Were you listening to me the whole time too?"

"Yes."

"And yet you asked me to repeat myself. If you can listen without hearing, you can certainly look without seeing. It's all right, you've got a lot going on." She turns and walks out of the room.

I look around the room. The bed has been made and all the clothes picked up. Either there's more to this than she's telling me or I'm the most unobservant person in the world. And right now, either (or both) is entirely possible.

Chapter Ten

Dad insists on us staying for lunch so he can talk with Aunt Guin—like he really cares about what I'm going to be doing this summer. Then he decides to give me some advice: Wear sunscreen; Wait an hour after eating before swimming; Neither a borrower nor a lender be. It's so obvious that he doesn't have a clue what to say. The only thing he says that's at all helpful is: Always go before you leave.

"That reminds me," I say, using the bathroom as an excuse to get away from him.

It's four o'clock before we're finally at the front door saying our good-byes.

"Let me go!" Billy says to me after I've been holding on to him for what he thinks is far too long.

It's not that I'm going to miss him that much. I mean, I love him and all that, but there's a limit. It's just that I don't want to say good-bye to Dad. I'd rather just walk away, but I know that isn't a possibility, so I hold on to Billy as long as I can. He's probably going to be the only one who misses me.

I try to will Dad's pager to go off so I can avoid the whole soon-to-be-ugly scene. While I'm holding Billy, it occurs to me that he hadn't known Mom for very long before she got sick, not long enough to remember what she was like when she was healthy. I wonder how much he will remember. The thought of him knowing The Creature better than Mom makes me shiver, and when I do, Billy stops squirming and rubs my back to warm me. I really am going to miss the little guy.

Mom was so different before the disease. Not as flighty as Aunt Guin—that wouldn't be possible—but she had her own energy. I remember that, but it's so vague, so distant. The cancer infected her body and my mind. It buried the good memories so deeply that, unless I'm dreaming, I need a photograph to remind myself of what she looked like before her skin turned gray. Most of the time I can't even remember farther back than the hospital. It hurts too much to remember her happy.

"You're going to miss me when I'm gone," I say to Billy as I let him go.

"Uh-uh," he says.

"Uh-huh."

"No, 'cause I'm coming with you."

"No, Billy. You're staying here with us," Dad says, quickly moving forward and gently but firmly putting his hands on Billy's shoulders.

"But I want to go with J!"

"I know, but I want you here with me."

Gee, Dad, can you tell me who your favorite is? I mean, don't hold back or sugarcoat it, just come right out and say it. Oh wait, let me.

"Yeah, Billy, he *wants* you." I pick up my backpack and turn to walk out.

"Jenevieve," Dad calls after me, leaving out the *you're being ridiculous* part of the sentence.

I turn around with a look that could rip through rock, and it does. I can see by the look on his face that he actually gets it! And there's no rock more solid than his head. How can a doctor be so stupid?

"Have a good summer," he says, almost apologetically.

"Oh, I'm sure it'll be peachy. Toodles!" I say with my biggest smile as I do a cheerleader twirl and get out of the house. Once out the door, I duck to the side and lean against the outer wall, wanting to be out of sight, but not out of earshot.

"She can be quite a handful," The Beast explains with fake sympathy.

"I guess that would depend on what else you're holding onto," Aunt Guin replies. "It was good seeing you again, Gerald, and meeting you, Fanny. Billy, I am eternally charmed."

"What's that mean?"

"That I think you're cool and next time you're coming with us."

"Promise?"

"Never trust anyone who makes a promise. Life has too

many curves to guarantee a destination. But I'll do what I can and that's quite a bit. You okay with that?"

"Yeah," Billy replies, sounding confused.

"I'll see you on Labor Day."

"See you then, Aunt Dibilybop," Billy says.

And before Dad or Fanny can say anything, Aunt Guin closes the door and walks past me.

"Well, come on," she says without looking at me. Her stride is strong and purposeful, and I have to jog to catch up and speed-walk to keep up. This goes on for a few blocks before I finally ask, "Where's your car?"

"What car?"

"The one we're taking to your cabin?"

"Oh, it's not a cabin, it's a house, and it's on a beach."

"I don't care…it's on a beach?"

"White sand."

"I'm too pale and skinny for a beach." I hate my body or lack of it.

"Tall and thin is in."

"Oh yeah, all teenage guys want to be with someone who's taller than they are."

"You don't strike me as the guy-chasing type."

"I'm not—at all."

"Okay."

"I'm not!"

"All right."

This is just infuriating. You say one thing—agghhh.

"So, where's your car?"

"What makes you think I have a car?"

She's joking. She has to be joking.

"How are we going to get to your house?"

"Hitch a ride," she says.

I stop. I think about the black veil camp. I think about spending my summer with an insane aunt. I think about my sore legs and about getting murdered by a psycho who drives around all day looking for hitchhikers. I think there must be another choice.

"I'm not hitchhiking."

"Why not?"

"Because we could get killed, raped, end up in the slave trade or get cut up into little pieces and sold as gourmet cat food."

"It's perfectly safe to hitch a ride as long as you know who's picking you up. It's a calculated risk that way, especially if you've arranged a time for said pickup." She looks at her watch and then up the road. "Right on time."

Chapter Eleven

I follow Aunt Guin's gaze to a vw van turning onto the street we're on. The van's seen better days. It's mostly silver but only because most of the paint is gone and the steel has been polished, except above the wheels where it's flesh toned—I think it's called body filler. The roof is cream colored, and I can only guess that's what the rest of it used to be. The sun reflects in waves off the van's side as it moves toward us like a steel caterpillar. Aunt Guin sticks her thumb out and the van pulls to a stop.

The driver, who looks about the same age as Aunt Guin, has long white hair tied back in a ponytail. His hairline points to blue sunglasses sitting on a little white nose. He leans out his window and removes what turn out to be sunglass clips, revealing violet eyes behind clear lenses in round wire frames. I quickly look down at the ground so that he won't catch me staring at him. I've never seen an albino before, and I don't want to be an insensitive jerk and stare at him like he's some kind of freak, because he's not—he's just different than normal people. Not that he's not normal…oh, this is awkward.

"Hello, ladies. Where would the two of you be off to today?" he asks.

Oh God, maybe he'll think I'm repulsed by him or something, and that's why I'm staring at the ground. I don't know if I can look without staring, though. What a horrible way to find out I'm an idiot.

"We're headed to Prince Edward County," Aunt Guin tells him.

"What a lucky coincidence! So am I. And what part of the county would you be going to?"

The way they talk to each other, it's as if they were putting on a show for me, mocking themselves as they speak, but they don't seem to be paying much attention to me at all. They seem more interested in entertaining themselves, which is fine. It lets me continue to stare at my feet.

"Why, out near Sandbanks Provincial Park."

"This is your lucky day indeed. That's where I'm headed."

"My name is Guinevere and this is my niece, Jenevieve, and we would be awfully grateful for a lift."

"Guin and Jen, lovely. I would be happy for the company. My name's Arthur, but you may call me Art. Tell me, Jen, is there something particularly fascinating about the patch of ground at your feet or is it the shoes that are demanding your undivided attention?"

Busted! I slowly look up and my eyes go to Aunt Guin first, to prepare myself or perhaps in hopes of rescue. She points to her eyes and then her mouth. I don't know why, but I wipe both my eyes and my mouth, just to be sure.

I look up at Art, and the first thing I notice is his mouth, which is curved up in the warmest and friendliest of smiles. Making my way up to his eyes, I find them gentle and playful with just a distant hint of sadness. I've never looked so closely at a person's smile or so deeply into their eyes before, but as I do, all our differences disappear.

"Nice to meet you, Jen," he says.

"Just J," I say, introducing myself properly. "And it's nice to meet you too."

"Hop in," he says as he pops open the side door. As nice as he is, I still don't feel comfortable getting into a stranger's van.

"If you know him, why did you introduce yourself?" I whisper to Aunt Guin.

"Every moment is the beginning of a new journey and another chance to reinvent oneself. Every time you introduce yourself, you start fresh. It makes it easier."

"Besides," adds Art, "think about how much stress and how many awkward moments could be avoided if you never had to remember anyone's name."

Oh no, there's two of them.

The van smells like gasoline. In the back there's a wall of freshly cut wood. They say that you can tell the age of the tree if you count the rings, so I count one of the rounds. It has close to thirty-eight rings. Maybe it was planted the year Mom was born. And died about the same time too. I try to picture the trees as they once stood, but I see only their dismembered bodies lying before me. As we make our way out of the city, the living trees can't take away the images of the remains. Seeing a seedling on one lawn, planted next to a stump, almost makes me sick.

The smell of dead trees overpowers the stink of gasoline and conquers my senses. It's the smell of death, and yet it's a pleasant smell—it's Christmas.

We used to make a big deal out of Christmas. Ours was always the largest tree on the block, and on Christmas Eve we'd invite the whole neighborhood over. The outside of the house would be covered in lights and the inside with tinsel and fresh-cut cedar boughs.

We live near a golf course, and Mom would go there at night with Billy, me, a toboggan and a pair of clippers. She'd cut branches off the cedars that line the course and I'd pile them on and around Billy, who stayed on the toboggan. He'd do his best to hold onto them. Mom loved the smell; she'd sniff the end of each one after she cut it. Dad used to play the course, so he pretended that he didn't approve, but he'd always tell Mom which trees needed trimming *if* she insisted on cutting them.

Everyone was at our Christmas parties. Not just people from the neighborhood, but people from my parents' work and my school friends too—back when I had friends. Mom would play the piano and sing Gordon Lightfoot's "Song for a Winter's Night." I'd tell her she was awful and that it was embarrassing. She'd tell me not to take things so seriously and to stop worrying about what other people thought.

Then she'd convince Dad to sing a duet of "Baby It's Cold Outside." I'd always make it clear to my friends just how mortifying I found it.

Mom loved to laugh and have a good time. Entertaining was her thing. She and my dad would do a dramatic reading of " 'Twas the Night before Christmas," acting out the different parts—complete with wardrobe and props—grabbing some unsuspecting person out of the crowd to spin around with at the "turned with a jerk" part.

It was the very definition of corny, but all the younger kids and the adults—with the help of a little rum and eggnog— loved it. My friends and I would watch from the sidelines, making sure always to be laughing at, and never with, them.

On Christmas morning, Mom would be up before any of us, even Billy. Dean Martin's "Silver Bells" blasting from the stereo would awaken the rest of us. She'd spray fake snow everywhere as we came down the stairs, and then we'd rip open the mound of presents. At least, I think that was us. I remember it all right, but not to touch, not to feel, just to watch, like an old film. Last Christmas—now *that* I can still feel with painful clarity.

There was no party, and there were no lights outside or cedar inside—only a touch of tinsel and a sad little tree for a sorry little Christmas. We all had to wait for Mom to wake up and for Dad to help her down the stairs to the chair by the fire. He wrapped her in a blanket, put a scarf around her neck and turned up the gas fireplace. He then straightened the knitted, pale yellow toque she'd been wearing since she lost her hair. After that he went into the kitchen, made her a cup of tea and handed it to her gingerly.

"Are you comfortable?" he asked her for the thousandth time.

"Yes, I'm fine. Just open your presents."

"You're sure?" he asked again.

"She's fine! Now can we get on with it?" I answered for her. Dad gave me a dirty look, but he didn't say anything.

I vividly remember Mom's frailty and how not even the fire's reflection could give her face any color. I remember Dad's patience and gentleness, Billy's enthusiasm, my anger. I watched all of it with a great fury, and I let that fury be known for the rest of the day. Why shouldn't I have been angry? I had lost my Christmas.

I got to be in the school's Christmas pageant, but I was the only one there without a parent. Dad arranged for me to get a ride with the neighbors and their kid, Martha.

Martha stuck to me all night like a bad smell—literally—and in doing so ensured the complete destruction of what remained of my social standing.

The thing about Martha, besides her "top student" marks and her random, loud, snorting laugh, is that she will occasionally stick her hand down the back of her skirt, pull it out and sniff it. She did it that night, *on stage*!

My perfect evening was complete when, on the way to the car, Martha grabbed *my hand* with *the hand*—Merry Christmas!

All I wanted was one morning—Christmas morning—just a couple of hours of normality. But Mom couldn't even give us that. How hard would it have been? One hundred and twenty minutes of pretending everything was all right. That was it. That was all I wanted.

"So are you a serial tree-killer or something?" It just comes out. I have no control. I need a distraction.

Art is talking to Aunt Guin, and from the way he jumps when I speak, I'd say he'd forgotten about me. I must have been zoned out for a while.

"What?" Art says. "Oh no. I'm a tree surgeon. I euthanize when I have to, but I save whenever I can. I'm bringing the wood with us for the campfire."

A campfire? Yee-haw.

"What do you do?" Aunt Guin asks me.

"I'm still in school—obviously—and if you're asking what I want to do when I grow up, I don't know."

"I mean what I say, and I say what I mean. School's not your passion. What do you enjoy doing?"

"I don't enjoy anything," I tell her. "I don't feel like talking anymore."

"Okay," Aunt Guin says, as polite as ever, not even acknowledging my rudeness. She turns to Art. "I can't wait to see the house. It sounds perfect."

"You haven't seen the house yet?" I ask, a little concerned.

"I thought you didn't want to talk," says Aunt Guin.

"I don't."

"Then I'm confused by the question, or more to the point…"

"And it's always good to get to the point," Art interjects.

"Oh, I couldn't agree more," Aunt Guin concurs. "Far too many people spend far too much time avoiding the issue…"

"Rambling on and on…," Art adds.

"About things that have nothing to do with what they're really thinking about…"

"While you sit there just thinking...," Art says.

"Come on, get on with it. I mean, really...," Aunt Guin says.

"The point being!" I could bear it no longer.

"Excuse me? Oh yes, the fact that you asked the question," Aunt Guin says.

"Perhaps," Art ponders, "she didn't mean to say that she didn't want to talk, but rather that she didn't want to answer."

"Ahh, some sort of game then...in which she only asks questions..." She turns to Art as Art turns to her.

"Twenty Questions!" they say together. They're far too excited for people their age.

"And what was the category?" Art asks.

Now if I were smart I would have cleared up this whole game-playing nonsense. But apparently I'm not quite as clever as I give myself credit for. "Your house!" I say, and then I quietly try to correct myself. "But I'm not..." Too late.

"Oh yes, I remember the question now. No," Aunt Guin replies.

"Why would you buy a house that you haven't seen?" I ask.

"EEEE!" Art makes a buzzer sound. "In Twenty Questions, only questions which can be answered with yes or no, or true or false, are permitted."

"What if it's infested with rats?" I ask.

"EEEE!"

"I'm not playing Twenty Questions!" I say, trying to make it as clear as possible.

"Really? We are," Aunt Guin informs me.

"Oh, this could make things tricky," Art says with genuine concern.

"Forget it," I say.

"Are you sure you want to give up so quickly?" Art asks.

"I'm sure," I tell him.

"My turn," Aunt Guin says.

"Topic?" Art asks.

"Animal."

"Does it have fur?"

"Yes."

I'm starting to think that Aunt Guin isn't as smart as I first thought.

"Can it dance?" Art asks.

"Maybe," Aunt Guin replies after careful consideration.

In fact, I'm starting to think she doesn't know much of anything, just like everyone else.

"Can it dance while people are watching?"

"No."

Their voices fade as I look out at the highway and my ears fill with the sound of rubber on asphalt and the engine hum that's thrown back at us from the large sound barriers.

I wonder what it's like beyond those barriers. Do they actually block out enough sound to allow you to forget what's on the other side? How high does the wall have to be? How thick? Where can I order one?

"A platypus?" Art asks Aunt Guin.

"Yes!" she replies.

Excited laughter is the last thing I hear as I let the van's motion carry me away to a much-needed sleep.

Chapter Twelve

The light of the late-afternoon sun is intensified by the van's windows and turns the inside of my eyelids from black to white, interrupting my slumber and forcing me to blink myself awake.

"It's beautiful," Aunt Guin says as she opens her door. It's only now that I realize the van has come to a stop. I hear a second door open, so I stretch and, with a few more blinks, clear my eyes.

I look out the window, but my eyes must not be fully adjusted. The house appears decrepit. There's a porch and a second-floor balcony held up by willpower and chipped paint; in fact, the whole house looks like it's held together by willpower and chipped paint.

"It is perfect, absolutely perfect," Aunt Guin raves.

"I thought you'd like it," Art says.

"It's ideal," she replies.

I keep blinking but nothing changes. I open my backpack to check for sunglasses. There's a pair inside the makeup bag, sitting right on top. I quickly put them on, but they don't improve the house's appearance. It must be the van's side window—please let it be the side window. Sliding the door open reveals a yard that is screaming out for abandoned cars and a beat-up RV. The yard is the deathbed on which the house lies.

"We're not staying here?" I ask as my stomach tightens.

"Of course we are," Aunt Guin replies.

"It's an abandoned house," I point out.

"Not anymore!" she says.

"A sneeze could knock it over," I say, only half joking. Well, not even half.

"Let's go inside, " Aunt Guin cheerfully suggests as she and Art move toward the death trap.

"I'm okay out here." Actually I won't be okay until I'm far, far away from here.

"Oh, come on. Remember, this is an adventure!"

"Our final one, I'm sure."

They disappear into the house and I reluctantly follow.

I make my way cautiously up the porch steps toward the structurally challenged house. With each stair, my step softens as the creaking gets louder. The whole house begins to whimper, begging me to stop.

Trying to will myself lighter, I think of nothing but feathers. At the top of the stairs, I stop and muster my courage to make it across the porch, which seems miles wide. The stairs are exhausted, ready to turn to powder from the strain that we've put them under.

"There's no turning back now," I tell myself, thinking of animals that get trapped on islands and ice floes during spring thaw. Pushing fear and wisdom aside, I gingerly move forward.

"Feathers, feathers, feathers." I'm halfway there. "Feathers, feathers, brick—oh no." With a loud crack the boards beneath me splinter and send me plummeting. Wood spears and rusty nails rip through both pants and skin and I come to a sudden ankle-shattering stop. I wince—the shock and intense pain take my voice away. Waist deep, I'm imprisoned by shards of wood that act like a medieval torture device. This is what it has come to, my tragic life cut short by shoddy craftsmanship. What could be worse? Then I feel it.

A rat crawls over my foot, dragging its six-inch tail. Its claws and dirty fur infect my wounds; its whiskers tickle my ankle; its little rat nose bobs up and down, sniffing at the cuts; its small black eyes grow larger and larger at the sight of blood. It starts to gnaw at me with its sharp little teeth. Another rat comes to join in the feast, and then another and another. Soon my legs are covered with them. My mouth opens, but still nothing comes out—betrayed by my own vocal cords.

"Come on, J, it's perfectly safe," I hear Aunt Guin say, and I look up to see that she's come back to the door to hurry me along.

Okay, so maybe there aren't rats and maybe the wood didn't break, exactly—or at all—but it could.

Once inside, the smell that fills my nostrils makes me realize it's unlikely there are any rats around. Judging by the aroma, whoever lived here before must have had about a million cats—or one cat with a *really* big problem.

"Oh my god! That smell! We can't stay here!" I say, since neither of them seems to notice.

"It just needs a little TLC," Aunt Guin says optimistically.

"Unless that means turpentine, lighter fluid and other combustibles, then I think you're aiming a little low."

Art laughs, which I like, even though it wasn't really meant to be funny.

"You have to look at what it could be," Aunt Guin says, her voice filled with optimism.

"An insurance claim." I'm on a roll, but Art isn't laughing this time. He is smiling though, but he's trying to hide it. I look over at Aunt Guin; she looks disappointed. What was she expecting? The place is a hole. Actually, a hole would be an improvement.

"I'll get your things from the van," Art says as he heads toward the door.

Aunt Guin looks at me.

"What?" I ask. "This place is a total disaster."

"You're looking at the flaws that lie without, instead of the potential that lies within. It's a solid house with a good foundation. It's just been neglected."

"It stinks."

"Okay, let's start with that." She looks around, inhaling deeply without throwing up, which is pretty impressive. Then she gets down on her knees and puts her nose right down to the stained, baby blue carpet. She inhales again and I think *I'm* going to throw up. "Yep," she says, "that's the source." She pulls a Swiss Army knife out of her pocket and cuts though the carpet, pulling up a corner. "Oak."

"That's good?" I ask.

"Yes, that's good," she says. "What else do you see?"

"I don't know," I say.

"Just look around and tell me what you see."

"Stained wallpaper to match the stained carpet, yellow trim—that I think started out white—an old fireplace with a god-awful green mantel. How could people live in this?"

"If you start thinking you're better than others, then it stands to reason that others are better than you. The universe doesn't play favorites," Aunt Guin says. "And besides, everything you mentioned is superficial. What I see are beautiful bay windows, nine-foot ceilings, maple trim underneath the paint, and a roaring fire under the cherrywood mantel."

"Are you starting to see the potential?" she asks. "Just let your imagination run free and listen to what the house tells you."

"What the house tells me?"

"Sure. It knows what it wants to be. You just have to encourage it a bit and it'll tell you; now listen."

I look and I listen to the house, and you know what the house tells me? Nothing. It's a house! It can't talk! I turn to point out this little fact, which she's apparently overlooked, when I'm stopped by her expression. You'd think she'd just walked into one of those homes out of *Martha Stewart Living* or *MTV Cribs*. She walks around, avoiding imaginary furniture and admiring the finished wood that lies under about six coats of paint. I decide to leave and she doesn't even notice. Outside, I see Arthur looking around the overgrown yard with the same stupid expression on his face as there is on Aunt Guin's. I head to the beach.

Chapter Thirteen

I arrive at the water as the sun slowly slips behind the bushes that stand watch at the top of the sand dunes about a kilometer away from the house. I head toward them. The beach behind the house is flat white sand, and it doesn't take long for my shoes to fill. I could go back and get the sandals that I'm sure Aunt Guin packed for me, but instead I just remove my shoes and socks. The sand feels hot but pleasant, massaging my feet with every step.

The disappearing sun turns the sky blood orange and promotes the sand to gold dust. Without the sun's heat, the sand becomes cool under my feet. I climb to the top of the dunes like a queen in her treasury room.

Near the top I sit to rest and admire the lake, now golden as well. It's hard to distinguish where the sand ends and the water begins. I push myself down into the dune, which is as formfitting as a giant beanbag chair.

From my perch, the house looks lonely and embarrassed. Its windows grab the colors of the sunset and hold them to distract from the peeling paint and overgrown garden, but the brilliant colors do little to improve it. The house looks like a vagrant with a marigold in his lapel.

Maybe it *can* talk. Maybe I just wasn't listening hard enough. Or maybe I'm losing my mind. I stare at the house, and I listen harder and harder. When I have a clear picture in my head, I close my eyes to try and heighten my other senses.

"Tell me what you want, talk to me. Speak, speak, tell me how you feel."

"Banzai!" The word blasts out over the dunes, echoing off the water. I spring up and open my eyes, and something hits me from behind, snapping my head forward.

"Banzai" turns into "aggghh" and then "ouch" as a boy goes tumbling over me and rolls down the dune. He digs his feet in and comes to a sliding stop about three-quarters of the way down. He shakes the sand out of his long, dirty-blond hair. At least I think it's dirty-blond, but maybe it's just blond and dirty. His face has sand stuck to it, but I can make out some freckles and sparkling green eyes.

"Cool," he says before looking up the hill to see what tripped him, which is how he finds me, still rubbing my head.

"Oh, sorry. I didn't know you were there."

"Well, I was," I tell him, which is a dumb thing to say.

"Yeah, I can see that now," he says, which is pretty much the only thing you can say back. "I really am sorry. Are you okay?"

"Aside from the whiplash, you mean?" I snap. "What were you doing?"

"Just jumping off the top of the dune."

"Why?"

"To see how far I could jump."

"Sounds like *loads* of fun," I say.

"You should try it! You just run as fast as you can and when you get to the edge, you jump. You're airborne for a few seconds, and then you slide into the sand. That is, of course, as long as you don't trip over someone. Then it gets a bit more complicated."

"So kicking a stranger in the head isn't usually part of it?"

"No, that's an added bonus."

He smiles. Through reflex alone, I smile back.

"Name's Connor," he says, climbing the dune and sticking his hand out as if he's been waiting a long time to meet me.

"I'm J," I say and put out my hand so as not to be rude. He shakes it firmly before plopping down at my side.

"You're not from 'round here, are you?"

"Unfortunately, no."

He nods and looks confused. Perhaps he's unfamiliar with sarcasm.

"Where you from?" he finally says.

"Toronto."

"Oh, boy, then you are lucky." Now I'm not sure, but I think he may be a bit more familiar with sarcasm than I first gave him credit for. "So what crime did you commit to get yourself sentenced here?"

Yep, he's familiar.

"My mom died and my dad didn't want me around."

"What an idiot...sorry."

"Don't be; he is one."

"I mean about your mom; the sorry part, not the idiot part."

"Oh, thanks," I say. Maybe he's not as bad as I first thought.

We sit there for a minute in silence, but the silence isn't awkward. We're just enjoying watching the sky go slowly gray as the world gets older.

"So are you at the campgrounds?"

"No, my aunt bought a house just over there."

"Which one?"

"The one that's crumbling," I say, pointing it out.

"I thought an albino bought that place. Is that your aunt?"

"That's not very nice."

"What?"

"Calling him an albino."

"Your aunt's a he?"

"No, the al...he's her friend."

"Oh, isn't he an albino?"

"He is, but it's not nice to say that."

"What's not nice about it? I can see calling a really pale white guy an albino might be considered an insult—and even that's questionable—but if you call an albino an albino...I don't see anything wrong with that."

"There is," I say.

He stops to ponder.

Now the silence is awkward.

"Do you know his name?" he asks.

"Whose?"

"The al...your aunt's friend?"

"Arthur, Art."

"Arthur Art?"

"Arthur, but he likes to be called Art."

"All right then. I thought Art bought the place."

"He bought it for my aunt—I think."

"Now we're getting somewhere," he says. "How long are you down for?"

"The whole summer," I say, expressing my excitement about the concept as clearly as I can.

"It won't be that bad. There's a lot of fun to be had in these parts."

"Like jumping off the top of the dunes?"

He smiles, more to himself than to me. It's kind of adorab...annoying. Annoying is what I mean—definitely.

"There's a dance hall buried in one of these dunes."

"No way!" I say.

"So way," he replies. "Moonlight Palace. The dunes shifted and buried it. They couldn't stop it because the government protects the dunes. They just had to sit back and watch it happen."

"How long ago?"

"I don't know exactly—in the fifties, maybe. Some of the locals say that the sand of the dunes stopped the sands of time, and if you can find the hotel and get inside, you'll be transported back to when it was still open and thriving."

"Really?"

"Really. Mind you, some of the locals drink a lot." He

glances over at the old house. "It looks like your aunt has a campfire going."

On the shore a fire burns brightly, and I can make out Art and Aunt Guin carrying some chairs to set around it.

"I'd better get back," I inform him.

"Yeah, me too," he replies, but I'm not sure if he really has to or if he's just saying that because I did. "I work at Vittles and Vitals—that's my parents' store—in the afternoon, so if you want to stop by, it's just a ten-minute bike ride from here."

"I don't have a bicycle."

"I can get you one, as long as you're not picky."

"That's okay."

"It's no trouble." He gets up and starts to walk back over the dunes from which he had so dramatically appeared. At the top he stops and turns around.

"Around here, people say things without thinking, so it's best to listen to what they mean instead of what they say. I didn't mean anything bad about your friend, though I can understand why you'd think so," he apologizes. "See ya," he adds, and then he disappears over the crest without waiting for a reply.

On the way back to the house, I think about what he said. I don't know why I got so upset about it. It wasn't like he used a derogatory term or anything. I wonder if Art gets offended if people call him that. I want to ask him, but I don't know if that would offend him. I wonder if even wondering about it makes me prejudiced. So I stop.

I start thinking about Moonlight Palace buried in the sand. How fast was it buried? Was there stuff still inside it?

Was it a big hall? Did it have a chandelier? And what about going back in time? Yeah, I know it sounds stupid, but what if?

A strong smell tantalizes me, and I look up to see that Art has a grill set up over the campfire. On the grill are a couple of steaks, a tofu something—I imagine it's Aunt Guin's—and potatoes wrapped in tinfoil. The smell of garlic hangs in the air.

"Where's the garlic?" I ask him.

"In the potatoes. Do you like garlic?"

"Mom used to cook with a lot of garlic."

"Is that a yes or a no?"

"I guess," I respond. I try and remain indifferent whenever possible. It makes it easier for me to change my mind without risking ridicule.

"Art, do you…?" I want to ask if being called an albino bothers him. I want to ask what it's like. I want to ask a lot of things, but all the words are stuck at the bottom of my throat, arguing with each other as to who's going to go first, all terrified of what they may face.

"Nothing," I finally say.

He smiles and checks the potatoes with a fork. "Okay."

"I mean…never mind."

"When words become land mines, even your allies have to watch their step. I assure you that this field has been swept."

"Do you mind being called an albino?" I blurt out.

"It all depends on which adjective is attached," he says, smiling. "It's not the word that offends, or at least it shouldn't be. It's the sentiment behind it."

"That's kind of what he said."

"Who?"

"The boy in the dunes."

"A boy in the dunes, eh?" he says, his smile now telling me there are more uncomfortable questions on the way— this time directed at me.

"There you are," Aunt Guin says, just in the nick of time. She's balancing a bottle of wine and a Coke on some plates. I jump up to help her.

"I was starting to get worried," she says.

"I thought you had too much faith to ever worry," Art says playfully.

"It's not faith that saves me but a complete lack of understanding," Aunt Guin says.

"Knowing you know nothing is the greatest under- standing of all," Art replies.

"So you're saying that by knowing I know nothing, I know everything there is to know. That's quite a paradox," Aunt Guin says.

"It'd have to be. One duck would never be enough."

Aunt Guin looks over to the grill. "I see you're having bull tonight."

"You can say that again," I say under my breath, but not far enough under, and they both look over at me, then back at each other.

"She may have a point," Art says.

"There's no way of knowing," Aunt Guin replies, and I catch them smiling.

Chapter Fourteen

After dinner we sit around the campfire. It hypnotizes me as I watch the flames closest to the wood sway gently while those farthest from the embers reach desperately for the sky. The occasional spark actually breaks away into the night to become one of the billions of stars that decorate the hemisphere.

I've never seen so many stars, and I find their infinity intimidating. Whenever I watch a movie that shows the night sky in the country, I always think it's digitally enhanced. Now that I see it, it could almost make you believe in heaven. It could almost make you believe in anything.

"J—J!" I hear a voice in the distance and turn to find Aunt Guin sitting right beside me. "Art's going to bed."

"What?" I ask as I slowly return from space.

I look over to see Art standing up and waving at me. I

get the feeling that he's been trying to say goodnight for some time.

Dazed, I watch as a friendly smile crosses his ghostly face. He almost glows in the firelight, and his eyes, framed by the flames' dancing reflection in his round wire glasses, look positively mystical. I find myself staring at him, not out of curiosity but wonder. His expression shows that he doesn't mind, he can sense the sentiment behind my gaze.

"Good night," he says, breaking the spell.

"Night," I reply.

He turns to Aunt Guin. "You're sure you don't want the van? I don't mind."

"No," she assures him. "We'll be fine out here."

The idea of sleeping outdoors should bother me, but it doesn't.

The warmth of the fire embraces me while the stars watch over me from far overhead. The crackle of the firewood keeps time for a lullaby of crickets and frogs. Waves roll in and the lake massages the sand. The world stops spinning and begins to gently rock back and forth. I want to stay right here—as long as it's not for more than one night, maybe two. There's only so much nature a girl can take.

With Art gone, Aunt Guin and I just stare at the fire in silence. Images start to appear in the flames, and the longer I stare, the clearer they become. Faces form, then bodies and then whole scenes start to play out. Some with Mom and they're not nice, they're...

"So, where's the washroom?" I ask, breaking my self-induced trance. Guin looks away from the fire and toward me. Her face is relaxed and she's glowing, but not from the flames. Not directly anyway. Whatever she saw in that fire must have been better than what I saw.

"Inside," she says calmly.

I look back at the house, where a light is on. Electricity, that's a surprise. But with or without light, the thought of what might be hiding or growing in the bathroom sends shivers through my body despite the fire's warmth. The sheer panic must show on my face.

"Don't worry," Aunt Guin says comfortingly, "I cleaned it."

I smile nervously, unwilling to believe anything in that house could ever become clean or even close to it. But I haven't used a washroom in ages, so I'm forced by my mortality to find a toilet—and fast.

"Where is it?" The fear in my voice makes Aunt Guin smile. I'm glad I can be such a constant source of entertainment.

"Right across from the living room. Just follow the clean smell."

I give a strained smile at her attempt at humor while cautiously making my way to the screened-in back porch that is eerily lit by a single yellow bulb.

My pace is set by a strange combination of fear, which holds me back, and a bursting bladder, which drives me forth. I think this was a tactic the British used to send troops into battle. They'd load them up on rum and tell them that the only washrooms were in enemy hands. Not that I'd had any rum. Just Coke.

I look up and see a small round attic window, which makes the house look like a Cyclops daring me to enter.

Unlike the stars, it isn't comforting. The closer I get to the house, the more I like nature.

Inside the screened-in back porch, I give my eyes a moment to adjust. The darkness in the country is so much darker than the darkness at home. Down the hall I see a sliver of light—my target. As my eyes refocus, I can see that the path between me and my goal is clear. I dash toward it. Once in the washroom, I close and lock the door. The bathroom is large, bright and spotless, judging by my thorough check of the toilet. No matter how badly I need to go, it's never bad enough to put my butt on a disgusting bowl. You could end up with an infection or something. But this bowl doesn't even require toilet tissue on the seat, and there is no need to hover.

While enjoying the release, I look around the room. Aunt Guin seems to have gotten into every crevice on the white tile floor and the blue tile walls. Both look clean despite the cracks and missing chips. The tub is long and deep; its sturdy feet look as if they could hold you up while you soak for hours. There's no shower.

In the corner of the room, a white washbasin and pitcher sit on a square, well-worn wooden table. The sink is a half-moon that's mounted on the wall, without a counter. There's a mirror above it but no medicine cabinet; there is no cupboard. I wonder where the people who lived here before kept their towels and stuff. I picture a tall cabinet next to the table, made from the same kind of wood in a similar design. As I finish up, panic sets in with the realization that there isn't a toilet-paper holder on the wall.

"Perfect, just perfect."

Looking up, I see a roll on the windowsill. I hate windows in washrooms; they make me nervous. Perhaps it could be changed to stained glass, with frosted glass put in the door to make up for the light that would be lost. While wiping, the picture of a multicolored, spiral-patterned mosaic floor comes to me. And then I flush.

As I open the bathroom door, I can see a flickering light coming from the living room. I must have been too concerned with peeing to notice it before. I go to investigate.

A fire sways beneath a cherrywood mantel. The hardwood floors are perfectly polished and reflect the flames, bringing the whole room to life. Burgundy walls set off the maple trim. A grand piano dominates the corner by the window. In front of the fire I see a brown leather chair with a matching couch next to it. The chair is large, and its arms invite you to curl up in it with a book and drift effortlessly into another world. There are framed classic-movie posters and paintings on the walls. There's no way all this could have been done today.

"Are you all right?" Aunt Guin calls from the outside door.

"How did you do that so quickly?" I turn to her to begin my interrogation. She won't get away with telling me that I wasn't paying attention this time.

"What?" she asks.

"The room."

"Just some bleach and elbow grease. Art helped."

I pause, trying to figure out her game. "I don't mean the bathroom."

"What then?"

"The…" I stop and turn back to the living room, but there is no fire, no cherrywood mantel, no furniture. It's just as it was when I first saw it, smell and all.

"J, what room?"

"Nothing," I yell back. "I'll be right out."

"You're sure you're all right?"

"I'll be right out," I repeat. The door closes while I stare into the empty room. It's lit by a vague trace of moonlight and bathroom light spillover. I think of the roaring fire and I wonder out loud, "Did she do that? Or was it the house?"

And then a third possibility crosses my mind.

"Or was it me?"

Chapter Fifteen

I awake shivering and run my hand down my clammy arm. The only blanket that covers me is the morning dew. Although the sun is high enough to wake me, it has yet to become hot enough to dry me out.

Aunt Guin walks toward me, holding my salvation in her outstretched hand. I get up to meet her and take the towel.

"I feel like a fish," I say.

"Good time to go swimming then," she replies, removing her dress to reveal a forties-style bathing suit. She runs and jumps into the water, carrying something in her hand. As she goes under, whatever she was carrying comes bobbing to the surface. I dry myself off.

"Well, come on," Aunt Guin says when she surfaces.

"That's all right. Don't much care for a swim first thing," I tell her as she grabs the unidentified floating object.

"What about a bath?" she says, rubbing her head. As

the foam appears, I realize the UFO was nothing more than a bottle of shampoo.

"Isn't that bad for the environment?" I ask.

"It's all natural; so is the soap," she says, grabbing a bar of soap out of a little mesh bag that was floating beside the bottle.

"I think I'll just use the tub."

"You can't. Not yet anyway. We have to let the water run for a while first."

"How long's a while?"

"Day or two anyway."

"Why?"

"Water's like the mind. If it's not used it becomes stagnant, even poisonous. It has to stay active to be kept healthy and clean."

"So, no drinking water?" Not that I don't appreciate the philosophy.

"I brought some with us. It's in the fridge."

I turn and walk toward the house.

"Aren't you coming in?"

"I think I'll skip it."

"You should start every day fresh," she says, rubbing her arms with the soap and watching the lather with great fascination.

I decide to share a little of my own wisdom.

"Just so you know, I'm never fresh first thing in the morning, especially when the morning starts first thing."

That being said, I turn and walk into the house. I can feel her smile on my back.

The fridge looks to be from the fifties, but it's clean, in

an off-white, well-aged sort of way. I open the door to find that, aside from an assortment of fruits and vegetables and the half-dozen liter-sized bottles of water, the fridge is empty. I grab one of the bottles and take three nice big refreshing gulps.

I didn't see Mom this morning. Apparently when you sleep outside there is no place between being asleep and being awake; you're either one or the other. I turn and look out the window. Aunt Guin's still playing around in the water. I hear the house door open.

"Mom?" I don't know why I say it, it just comes out. For a second, a split second, I forget.

As Art enters the kitchen, I feel tears form in the corners of my eyes, but I hold onto them with all I've got.

He comes in carrying a basket. He stops at the door and looks at me with a sympathetic smile, but there's no pity in it, for which I'm grateful.

"You okay?"

I nod, holding my breath to help with the tears.

"I got some fresh-baked rolls at the shop down the road. I think they're Pillsbury, but it's the thought, right?"

I force a smile.

"Guin swimming?"

I nod, biting my lower lip.

"I'll go out and see her," he says awkwardly. He's not really sure what to do, and I can't open my mouth to tell him to go.

Mercifully, he leaves, but on his way out he rubs my back and knocks a couple of the tears loose, sending them tumbling down my face and into my mouth, filling it with the salty taste of the chips Mom used to buy me.

The second memory-ambush breaks through my weakened defenses, crippling me. My own body uses chemical warfare against me as the salt drains the moisture from my mouth. I'm choking, struggling for a new breath. I force myself to inhale deeply. The sweet smell of early summer comes through the open kitchen window, passing through my nose and filling my lungs. The smell almost rescues me, but then I am assaulted with a scent that destroys any thought of a healthy, living Mom and replaces it with the smell of the funeral parlor. I really hate lilies.

My stomach tightens; something wants to get out. I run deeper into the house, praying for the smell of cat urine, anything but this death-pollen, which coats my throat and gags me. I race to the bathroom and stick my face over the toilet. The smell of chlorine is too late to save me, and my body contracts. There is no little pickle to distract me this time. The only thing my body is trying to expel is every memory of Mom's gray skin.

My stomach wrenches and wrenches, trying to get rid of the gray so that only her perfect pinkness will prevail. It even tries draining my color away to give it to her as the dry heaves make me pale and light-headed, but all the images in my head remain charcoal sketches—colorless, meaningless, void of all but emptiness, if that's even possible.

I fall to the floor and curl up in defeat. The exorcism has failed, and the gray that devoured Mom shows its power by lingering in every memory I have of her. I wonder how long it will be before it starts eating away at me.

～

I come out of the house in my bathing suit. It's not my favorite one. I guess Aunt Guin isn't all that perfect. She gets out of the water and wraps a towel around herself. I don't see Art anywhere.

"You've decided on a swim after all."

I have to wash the salt off my cheeks, I think, but give only a shrug in reply.

I dive into the water before she gets a good look at my face. The water is cool enough to be refreshing but warm enough to be comfortable. As it envelops me, the world disappears.

I love the water, the way it touches every part of you at the same time. Why the Little Mermaid would trade in a life underwater for a pansy prince in tights is beyond me. The water caresses my stomach like a thousand tiny little hands, a thousand tiny slimy little hands. That's not the water, that's…eels! I rush toward the surface. The eels wrap themselves around my feet, trying to pull me under. I emerge with a scream.

"What's the trouble?" Aunt Guin yells from the shore with far too little concern in her voice.

"Eels!" I scream.

Looking puzzled, she tilts her head.

"There's eels!" I yell again, trying to fully relay the gravity of the situation.

Her head now tilts the other way.

"Under the water—eels!" I repeat.

The lack of required panic promotes her from silly to stupid.

"It's only seaweed," she says.

"Seaweed!" Better than eels, but still. "It's grabbing my feet."

"It's just being friendly."

"Well, I'm not!"

"So swim out of it."

It annoys me when people point out the obvious, especially when I don't see it first.

I swim out of it easily, but remnants remain wrapped around my feet, sending nails-on-a-chalkboard shivers up my spine. It takes forever to get to shore, trying to kick the seaweed off while swimming.

"Ew, Ew, Ew," I moan as I make my way to dry sand and begin picking the strands of sea snot off my legs. "I could have drowned!"

"How's that?" Aunt Guin asks.

"If the seaweed hadn't broken away; if it pulled me under."

"It doesn't pull, it just stands there swaying in the current. It's really rather Zen."

"So's a corpse, and that's what I would have been."

"A corpse may be relaxed, and decomposition would certainly make it one with the universe, but it's not really Zen because…"

"I could have died!"

"The panic does you more harm than the seaweed," she tells me, "and if you realize you're only in the seaweed for a microsecond, then there's no reason to panic."

"A microsecond? What if I was really tangled? It could have taken me five minutes or more to get out of it. I would have been a goner for sure."

"No, no one could be tangled up for five minutes. That *is* impossible."

"I'm glad we agree."

"Yes and no. We said the same thing, but we meant different things."

"What?"

"*You* meant it's physically impossible to be tangled for five minutes without panicking or even drowning."

"Yeah," I say, leaving out the *that's pretty obvious* part of the sentence.

"*I* meant it's cosmically impossible for five minutes to exist."

It's barely breakfast time and she's already out to lunch.

"The past is gone, the future doesn't exist; it's only the moment that's real, lasting but a microsecond before it's new again. You can do anything for a microsecond."

And that lunch was one wing short of a party platter.

She was starting to seem a little smug, so I thought I should point out her lack of perfection.

"I prefer my other swimsuit, by the way. Not that it matters. I just thought you should know."

"You don't want to take your favorite swimsuit to the beach," she replies. "The sand will wear it out too quickly."

I should have known.

"I'm going for a walk," I say.

Chapter Sixteen

Two weeks ago today I still had a mother. Or the remnants of one anyway, since, in truth, she was closer to death than she was to life. Why is death so random, so cruel? If God wants it to be on earth as it is in heaven then why can't every day be Judgment Day? A day when the wicked die so that the good can live? And why did death take my mother so slowly? What sin did she commit that she had to suffer for?

"At least she's not suffering anymore," people say, thinking it will comfort me. She never should have suffered in the first place. I want her back as she was before, before any of this... viciousness that was thrown upon us by an apathetic god.

"At least you got to say good-bye," others say. Like her drawn-out suffering was some kind of blessing. That's like saying that it's best to be tortured before you die. That way you can see it coming.

No one gets to say good-bye. It's not some kind of love-in, where everyone sits in a room filled with flowers, sunshine and scented oils, holding hands, savoring the last moments that they have together, telling one another how much love they feel, the love becoming *so* complete, *so* pure, that it creates a burst of light and angels swoop in and fly the dying one's soul off to heaven. That's not the way it was at all.

The hospital room was cold, dark and dismal. The fluorescent lights made Mom's gray skin a pale, almost puke, green, which was rather fitting, really.

I didn't tell my mother how much I loved her. I didn't even tell her that I was going to miss her. She was too drugged to tell me anything. Her body had already started to decompose, full red lips becoming thin, brown, dry and chapped. Perfect cheekbones made ugly by sunken cheeks, her soft strong hands weak and skeletal.

The emotional energy didn't fill the room; it drained it. And it wasn't love. At its best it was fear and confusion, but mostly it was anger and hatred toward everything and everyone. Toward my mother for leaving, my father for letting her go, my brother for not understanding, the doctors for not doing more, the nurses for not caring enough and the janitor for cleaning the halls like it was any other day. It wasn't any other day. It was the day my mother died.

Fourteen days have gone by since that day. But it feels like one day, and at the same time it feels like a lifetime has passed. Which it has.

I haven't talked to my father or brother in a week. They're three hundred kilometers away and, by now, sharing the house with a bunch of flying monkeys. I've been whisked away by an insane aunt and an albino philosopher who, though not as extreme a case as my aunt, does appear to be a little reality challenged. They brought me to a decrepit house, miles from the civilized world. Not much of a rescue.

The only saving graces are the lake, the sand dunes and maybe Connor. The jury's still out on Aunt Guin and Art.

I lie on top of one of the dunes and watch a lonely little cloud float overhead. It blocks the sun and paints me gray. I think of Mom and I wonder…

"What are you doing?" I hear a familiar voice say.

I arch my back slightly to get my head back far enough to see Connor's face. His hair flops over his forehead, and even though there is a shadow across his face, I can still see the bright green of his eyes.

"Do you want to kiss me?" I ask.

I have no idea where the words come from. I just want to forget the pain and feel something other than loss. Since throwing up doesn't seem to work, maybe kissing Connor will.

But I've never kissed a boy before, and if he gave me a second to think about it, I would take it back. I don't get a second.

He's on me like a lion on a gazelle. At first contact, his lips pressed against mine feel good, but then I push him and the feeling away as my grief returns on a wave of nausea, my body tingling with guilt before numbing again.

I'm sorry, Mom.

I manage to hold down my vomit so as not to hurt Connor's feelings. His face fills with silent apologies; his lower lip completely disappears, as if it's too embarrassed to show itself. "Do you know where Moonlight Palace is?" I ask, longing for a distraction.

His lower lip cautiously reappears.

"The general area, not the exact spot, but I know about it, I mean—well, I know…actually, no, I have no idea. But I'm up for a quest," he says enthusiastically.

I hope it's the change of topic that's getting him excited.

"A quest it shall be then," I say as I get up, relieved that he didn't mention the…

"J," Connor says, "about what just…"

"What?" I say while shooting him a *don't go there* glare.

"Nothing," he says.

"You mean the nothing that never happened?"

"Okay," he says.

"Yeah," I tell him. "We're never going to speak of that nothing again."

"Okay," he repeats, sounding both relieved and disappointed.

I smile to let him know that everything's all right.

Chapter Seventeen

Instead of walking along the beach, we go down the back of the dunes, feet sliding on every step, which is great when you're going down and really tiring when you're going up. Ascending, you feel like you're getting farther away from the top with every step, like the earth itself is trying to stop you from getting there. Descending, you're pulled down with every step, the way Billy tugs on my sleeve and pulls me around when we're in a toy store and he sees something that he wants.

"This way, this way," the dunes say, dragging me down toward the trees that are both welcoming, with their outstretched limbs, and ominous with the darkness that lies between them.

We enter the forest, which isn't as dark as it first appeared. Instead of night's blackness, the woods are filled with evening shadows that dance playfully, safe from the afternoon sun until twilight comes and allows them to leave the forest's boundaries.

My hearing sharpens in the forest; every twig snap has digital clarity. I think of the creatures all around me, cowering at the sight of humans the way humans cower from the criminally insane. Are humans the bogeymen of the animal kingdom?

Do the Mommy and Daddy animals tell their children stories about the evil humans who will come and snatch them if they don't behave? Do the little ones dare each other to see how close they can get to the humans? Is that why animals scurry at the sight of us?

A thousand unseen eyes are upon me, and I wish I were one of them so I could run to my burrow and hide from the scary humans who are capable of anything and everything.

"Have you ever wished you were a cat?" I say, needing to break the painful silence.

"You mean like a cougar or a lion?"

"Any kind."

"I don't think I'd like to be a house cat—they're too helpless," Connor says.

"It looks like a pretty good life to me. Lying around all day, having someone tend to your every need."

"Being kicked around, having your tail lit on fire by some psycho who wants to feel powerful."

"You're starting to scare me now," I say.

"I only mean a house cat's life relies too much on the kindness of its owner. I'm sure your cat has a wonderful life."

"It would if we had one. We had a dog once." I decide to spare Connor the story of Spiral.

Connor pulls a small bag out of his pocket.

"Tootsie roll?" he asks.

"No thanks," I reply, turning away as he bites down. "My mom said I could have a cat when I got older, but then she..." I'm tired of saying it, so I don't.

After the appropriate moment of silence, Connor continues, "You should get one."

"My dad will never go for it. He doesn't believe in putting money into anything with a heartbeat, which is funny, considering he's a doctor."

Connor stops and looks up at the sky. We've been wandering for a couple of hours at least, and it doesn't feel like we're going in any particular direction.

"I'd better get going," he says. "I have to work this afternoon."

"But we haven't found Moonlight Palace."

"If we found it today, what would we do tomorrow?"

He has a point.

Chapter Eighteen

When I open the door, I'm welcomed by the smell of berries and I see the row of scented candles climbing the staircase. I hear dull thuds and what sounds like something falling. I follow the sound to the living room.

Aunt Guin's beautiful hair is now all tucked up under a hard hat. She's wearing a pair of denim overalls and a once-white T-shirt, some big ol' work boots and a leather tool belt complete with a hammer as an accessory. For makeup, her whole face, except for around her eyes and mouth, is covered in a thick layer of dirt—as is the rest of her body for that matter. Art is in much the same condition.

"It's renovations—you've got to get a little dirty," Aunt Guin says with a smile.

"You look ravishing," Art teases.

"Maybe we'll get the *GQ* cover," Aunt Guin jokes.

I look up and see the ceiling is no longer solid. It's now a bunch of thick bare wooden beams running across the top of the room, holding up the upstairs floor.

"Stop looking at my bare bottom!" I hear the house say, and I quickly avert my eyes. It talked to me! It was rather snippy, but it talked to me!

Art and Aunt Guin load up a wheelbarrow with the ceiling debris, which covers the floor. I look to the corner of the room, where I spot two pairs of goggles and two face masks on a ladder beside a camera on a tripod.

"What's the camera for?" I ask.

"We're making a renovation show, going to call it *Top to Bottom*. What do you think?" Aunt Guin asks.

If you're referring to the direction that my life has taken, then it's perfect.

"Shouldn't you have a cameraman?" I ask.

"I'm mainly doing it as a promotional video for myself, but I might try and sell it to TV. Wouldn't that be great?"

"That would be great," I agree, with all the exuberance of a kid thanking her grandmother for the socks and under-wear at Christmas. "Do I have a place to sleep yet?"

"On the beach."

"Lovely." I continue through the house toward the back door so I can go and pretend I have privacy in my imagi-nary room.

"Would you like to help us with the renovations? It'd speed things up."

"I would," I yell back. "But there's all those pesky child labor laws and I wouldn't want to be the cause of any law-suits. Thanks for asking though."

"Why don't we break for lunch?" I hear Art say.

"I talked to your dad again," Aunt Guin calls to me. "He wants you to phone him."

Yeah, well there are a few things I want him to do too, and none of them include a phone—unless you get really imaginative.

"You can use Art's cell phone," she says. "It's on the counter in the kitchen."

"Fine," I say, knowing I can't put it off any longer.

"Hello, Billy speaking."

"Hi, Billy," I say.

"J!"

"You don't have to yell, Billy."

"Whatcha' doin'?" he says at the same elevated volume.

"Just talking to you," I say.

"I'm talking to you too," he replies, his voice filled with the excitement of being able to talk on the phone.

"It's just a regular conversation, " I say.

"Yeah," Billy says. "I miss you."

"I miss you too."

"Hello," Dad says. He's taken the phone from Billy—like he always does.

"Hi, Dad."

"J, is everything okay?"

"Yeah, Dad. I'm just calling you back like you asked."

"Good," he says, already struggling for words. "I just wanted to be sure that everything was okay."

"Couldn't be better. The house is beautiful and my life is now complete."

"Good," he says. "It's good to hear your voice."

"From a distance," I say under my breath.

"Sorry?"

You should be.

"Nothing," I say.

"Oh," he says. "Things are good then?"

"Yes."

"Good," he says, followed by a long pause.

"How's The…Fanny?" I ask.

"Fine." Another long pause. "J."

"Yeah."

"Uh…be true to yourself."

"What?"

"You know…be uhh…"

"Yes, Dad, I know, and I'll be sure to look both ways before I cross the road."

"That's good. And call me…every night."

"Every night?"

"Well…often."

"I will."

"That's good."

"Lunch is ready," I tell him. "I gotta go."

"Okay, then. I'll talk to you again soon."

"Okay, bye."

"Jenevieve," he says urgently, as if he thinks I've already hung up, and if he calls out I'll somehow hear him and we'll reconnect.

"Yeah, Dad."

"Umm…be sure to brush."

"I will, Dad." I give him a few seconds, just in case he's thought of any other pearls of wisdom to offer.

"Bye," I finally say.

"Bye," he replies.

It'd be funny if it weren't so painful.

We have burgers for lunch. Soy burgers or, as I like to call them, *joy* burgers, 'cause they're just so darn much fun!

"You need a well-balanced diet," Aunt Guin says. "And soy is awfully good for you."

I completely agree with the awful part.

After lunch, Aunt Guin asks again, "You sure you don't want to help? I think you might like it."

Oh yeah, looks like a blast.

"What would I have to do?" I ask, to humor her.

"Hit things."

I'm listening, but that's all she says.

"You just want me to hit things?"

"Yep."

"All right."

And that's what I do. I put on a pair of jeans, a jacket, a pair of heavy work boots, thick gloves, a mask, safety goggles and a hard hat—an outfit that reminds me of an ant's exoskeleton (I was right about calling it a site). Art hands me a heavy steel bar with a hook on the end. Then he points to the wall.

"Go to town," he says as he starts to hit the wall with a similar bar.

That should be easy, I think as I follow his lead.

I hit it and hit it as bits of plaster and wood go everywhere. Out of the corner of my eye I see that Art has stopped hitting and gone back to helping Aunt Guin clean up. Occasionally he cleans the lens of the camera, but I pay little attention. I just keep hitting and hitting and thinking of everything—Mom's cancer, Dad's uselessness, Billy's obliviousness, the doctors, the nurses, the janitor and Fanny. I think a lot about Fanny.

I don't take a break. I don't even take the water that Art offers me. I just keep hitting. When I'm done, the vertical wall beams are as bare as the horizontal ceiling ones. "Cover me, cover me!" the beams cry out. "This is just so humiliating."

And I smile.

I walk outside for some fresh air and I keep walking, increasing my pace as I cross the road, and then my walk turns to a run, the heavy boots losing their weight as I run through the adjacent wheat field.

I don't stop as much as collapse. My arms are sore, my hands tingle, but I feel great. I inhale deep and long, enjoying all the scents of summer in the country—sweet, light and pure. Getting back on my feet, I turn around to look at the house.

The sun is hiding behind it like a child playing peek-a-boo—thinking that since it can't see me, I can't see it. I start to realize how long I was swinging that bar and why my arms are ready to fall off.

The sun's rays backlight the disheveled home, taking away many of its flaws by highlighting the beauty of its frame, its proud structure. It was once the pride of the block—if you call it a block out here. I can see it as it once was and, like Aunt Guin, I can see what it could be.

But as I walk back, the closer I get to the house, the

more the flaws emerge. Everything is beautiful if you don't get close to it. Maybe that's why God doesn't interfere; he's not close enough to us to see that anything's wrong. Or maybe he sees the perfection and knows that it's up to us to maintain or destroy it. I wish I knew. Oh, how I wish I knew.

Chapter Nineteen

Ching ching. Ching ching. Last night I had a dreamless sleep. I didn't get to enjoy the campfire or the stars. I had my dinner, closed my eyes, and now—*Ching ching. Ching ching*—this annoying noise—*Ching ching. Ching ching*—awakens me.

"Stop!" I demand.

"Morning, sleepyhead." I hear a familiar voice and open one eye a sliver to see Connor, high above me. "You're looking especially cute today," he says.

The statement is embarrassingly forward. The kiss is obviously not forgotten. I'm about to set him straight when I see that his expression lacks any seriousness, and I recall that I didn't even clean up before going to bed.

The morning dew, which I slept through, probably turned the thick layer of plaster dust and grime into mud, and the sun dried it again. I can't even imagine what I look like, but judging by his wide grin, I can imagine it's quite amusing—to him anyway.

"Ha, ha!" is the extent of my wit first thing in the morning. I close my eyes, hoping that if I can't see him, he can't see me.

"You look like you've been mud wrestling."

"Hee, hee." I'm getting sharper.

"It's kinda hot."

"Shut up!" I yell and jump to my feet, ready to *give 'em what for*—as Aunt Milly would say—when I see the source of the *ching ching*: a little silver bell that's attached to the handlebars of an old, but seemingly functional, blue three-speed woman's bicycle.

"It's for you," he informs me.

"You bought it for me?"

"No," he says, leaving out the *get over yourself* part of the sentence. "It's my mom's, but she doesn't use it anymore."

"Why not?"

"She's too fat."

"That's not nice."

"No, it's not nice at all," he says. "But all she eats are fries and hot dogs and all she drinks is pop, so it's the natural outcome."

The sentiment is loving, even though the comment is kind of cruel.

"So do you want to go for a ride?" he asks, indicating a boy's bike, equally beaten up.

"I better check with my aunt."

"It's okay," says a voice from the back porch, and I look

over to see Aunt Guin through the screen, wearing a large grin.

She's been watching the whole time, I'm sure.

Art steps out of the house, and he's smiling too—I hate that.

I give them an exaggerated mock smile in return and go to grab the bike, but my arms feel like weights are tied to them.

It takes all I've got to grab the handlebars and push the bike out of the sand.

"Don't be too late," Aunt Guin says, her smile widening.

"I have to work at one o'clock, so we'll be back before then," Connor informs her.

I try to ignore them all.

I throw a change of clothes in a bag and we hit the road, heading to a different part of the beach, having decided that looking in the woods for a dance hall buried by sand is not our best course of action. From now on, we'll stick to the dunes.

When we arrive at the park, we can't get all the way to the dunes with our bikes, so we stuff them in between a couple of trees.

"Won't they get stolen?" I ask.

"Out here?" Connor says. "Nah." Then, looking at the condition of the bikes, he adds, "Who'd want them?"

We both pick a good walking stick—after checking several for the right combination of height, weight and strength—and start making our way to the beach.

Standing at the top of one of the dunes, I make Connor

go to the bottom while I turn one of the bushes into a change room. I get out of the filthy clothes—some of which are sticking to me after the bike ride—and slip into my bathing suit. Connor occasionally looks up and over his shoulder, trying to sneak a peek. I can see him, but I know by his look of disappointment that he can't see me.

I run down the dune past Connor, dropping my bag of clothes and walking stick before diving into the water. I stay under, scrubbing my face to try and get as much guck off it as possible. I emerge long enough to see Connor kicking his shoes off. I go back under and start to work on my hair. I can feel bits and pieces of the nasty living room wall clinging to my scalp. I wish I'd brought Aunt Guin's shampoo with me. I would have asked, but I wanted to get away from the Cheshire cats as quickly as possible.

I come up again. Connor's face is inches from mine. I kick away from him.

"What are you doing?" I ask.

"I thought you might be drowning."

"I'm not!"

"All right," he says, backing away.

I may have been a bit harsh, but I don't apologize. I can feel seaweed against the bottoms of my feet; I don't mind it this time. I even use it to try and get the dirt out from between my toes.

"Only for a microsecond."

"What?" Connor asks.

"Only for a microsecond. It was something my aunt said. The past is gone, the future doesn't exist. All that's real is the moment, which lasts only for a microsecond. You can do anything for a microsecond," I say, doing my best Aunt Guin impersonation.

"'The distinction between past, present and future is a stubbornly persistent illusion,'" Connor says.

"What?" I ask.

"Einstein said that."

"You read Einstein? You quote Einstein?" I say, more than a little surprised.

"I watch a lot of science fiction," he says, shattering my newly formed illusion.

I laugh. Connor doesn't look amused.

"People highly underestimate the educational value of movies and television. Especially science fiction," he says defensively.

I laugh harder, but it's not at him.

Connor doesn't know that though, and he turns and starts to swim to shore.

"Stop," I yell after him. "I'm not laughing at *you*."

He turns around to face me. "No? What are you laughing at then?"

I can't reply, because I don't know what I'm laughing at, and realizing that I don't know makes me laugh all the harder. It's quite a strange feeling, laughing; my stomach will probably hurt tomorrow.

Connor turns away again.

"No, stop, really, please." I get it under control.

He turns back to me.

"Thank you," I say—I meant to say sorry, but it was thank you that came out.

"For what?"

"Just thank you," is all I can reply.

He looks at me, confused. I would look at me confused too. Connor swims toward me. A head bobs along the top of the dunes, like a puppet.

Connor reaches me.

"There's somebody up there," I tell him, and he spins around and looks.

"No there isn't," he says, spinning back. "It's the sun playing tricks."

I don't like being told I'm imagining things, and my look tells him so. He smiles apologetically, but his smile's got a bit of condescension to it too, because he still doesn't believe me.

"It looked like someone with a mullet," I say, to add substance to my "vision."

Connor's eyes get bigger and worry transforms his face.

"My brother!" he says, quickly turning and swimming to shore.

"What?" I yell after him.

After making our way back to where we'd left the bikes, we stand side by side, looking up. I've put shorts and a T-shirt on over my swimsuit, but they won't do much to protect me from the fir needles, and I have no intention of putting the dirty clothes back on.

"My brother," Connor repeats.

"How'd he get them up there?" I ask, looking to the top of the thirty-foot Douglas fir—the kind we always got for a Christmas tree. Our bicycles hang like ornaments near its peak.

Connor shakes his lowered head and mumbles, "Probably had his monkey do it."

I don't ask.

Connor walks to the base of the tree and starts climbing.

"Can't you just teleport them down?" I say. This time the laugh *is* at Connor's expense.

Chapter Twenty

Connor rescues both bikes but gets covered in cuts and scrapes in the process. Seeing him all sticky and cut up makes me feel bad about the poor timing of my sci-fi joke, and I apologize to him when he leaves me at my aunt's to go to work. He'll forgive me—eventually.

That afternoon, and every afternoon that follows, I help with the house's restoration, though resurrection would be a more apt term; we're bringing the house back to life and out of isolation.

Most evenings we spend on the beach. Aunt Guin invests in a tent to protect us from the morning dew.

There are few rainfalls, so we keep the tent's mesh sunroof open almost every evening, and I fall asleep under the stars' watchful gaze. She also buys a portable stereo that we listen to while we work.

Art plays the guitar around the campfire at night and

Aunt Guin sketches caricatures of us. She's promised to do a painting for me on a "grander scale," whatever that means. Connor sometimes comes for dinner when he's done helping in the store, and sometimes I go over to his place. Connor also plays the guitar. I discover this when he plays "If You Could Read My Mind," one of my favorite Lightfoot songs.

"I'm surprised a city girl has even heard of Gordon Lightfoot," Connor says with a cheeky grin.

I reply by rolling my eyes.

He then plays another Lightfoot song, the one Mom used to play at the Christmas parties—"Song for a Winter's Night." It seems almost surreal hearing it on a beach in the middle of summer.

From the dunes, I could swear I hear the sound of a piano, and I close my eyes to try and picture Mom playing it. Nothing comes but a cold shiver like snow falling on my bare skin. A flake lands in the corner of my eye and melts, tracing a line down my cheek.

I open my eyes and Connor warms me with a smile. The corners of my mouth rise with unexpected ease as I return his sign of affection.

The laughter that Connor gave me lasts throughout the summer. I even share it with Art and Aunt Guin when I try to participate in some of their bizarre word games.

My weekly phone calls to Dad and Billy get less painful as each week passes more quickly than the last.

Like the sparks that broke from the fire to become stars, my summer is turning into a collection of fleeting moments that scatter themselves like points of light filling the void of my life.

Though we all help each other out, Aunt Guin is in charge of the house's interior salvation. I get to offer suggestions on all areas of the remodeling, inside and out. Art is mainly responsible for the exterior.

At Aunt Guin's insistence, I expand my musical horizons. When you share the same CD player while you work, musical tastes can become a problem.

I take some of the money she pays me and, on one of our trips into town, invest in a Gordon Lightfoot tribute CD—one step at a time—which leads me to buy Ron Sexsmith's *Cobblestone Runway*, which leads to Coldplay, which then leads me to other music that the kids at school might even consider "cool." I don't let that discourage me.

When Aunt Guin gets her turn at the stereo, we listen to world music, stuff like African drumming or Balinese gamelan music, which sounds like a garage band playing wind chimes.

Art's musical preference is classic rock, but he's very easygoing so he doesn't often get his choice. He originally wanted to listen to country music, but Aunt Guin and I immediately put the kibosh on that.

"I thought you of all people would be more open-minded about music," Art says to Aunt Guin in defense of his musical selection.

"Everyone has a line that they don't care to cross," Aunt Guin says, "and country music is mine."

Art turns to me, looking for support.

"You know," Art says to me, "if you like Gordon Lightfoot, you should really give country music a try."

"Gordon is *not* country," I tell him. And it is never mentioned again.

～

With the rhythm of tribal drums and what sounds like a squirrel being ironed coming from inside the house, a chill goes through my body as I find myself almost liking it. Maybe I've just built up an immunity to it over the summer. Yeah, that must be it.

I look over at Art, who's wearing his blue sunglass clips under a Shady Brady straw cowboy hat. The hat's name suits it since it keeps Art's face and neck in constant shade. What if he'd gotten to listen to country? Would I have found myself almost liking...oh, I can't even go there.

With the yard cleaned up, gardens planted and the trees all perfectly trimmed, Art helps me with the painting. He puts the finishing touches on a green shutter while I work at making the rest of the house sparkling white.

He's so focused and quiet when he works, never forcing a conversation or a game.

"Art?" I say. "You're not as weird as Aunt Guin—at least not when she's not around."

Art laughs. "You think your aunt's weird?"

"In a good way. I mean, I really like her," which is true, "it's just, you seem a bit more..."

"Boring," he says.

"No, " I assure him. "You're just more, well...normal."

"That's what I said—boring," he says, and then he smiles at me to let me know he's half joking. "Your Aunt Guin and I knew each other in university. We were in the same philosophy class. When we get together, I slip back into post-secondary playfulness."

"What was she like in university?"

"Same as she is now. Your aunt's always been a free spirit."

"I didn't meet her till my mom died."

"I know."

"Do you know why?"

"That's something you'll have to ask her," he says.

"Where are you from, Art?" I ask.

"Toronto. I live there with my wife and kids."

"You have kids?"

"Don't sound so surprised!"

"I'm not...I just..."

"A boy and a girl," he continues, letting me off the hook. "Eight and ten. They're with their mother and her family in Poland for the summer. I could have gone, but when Guin called and wanted me to go in with her on finding a house to fix up and sell, I said yes. And to be honest, a summer with my in-laws didn't really appeal to me."

"Your wife doesn't worry about you spending the summer with another woman?" I ask.

"No," he says with a chuckle, the reason for which is unclear.

"Why...wait. Did you say Aunt Guin's going to sell this place?"

"That's what she does. Finds places in need of restoration, brings them back to their former glory—and usually a bit more—and moves on."

I don't know why, but this information gives me a sinking feeling.

"But she ordered furniture; it's coming next week."

He shrugs his shoulders. "She knows what she's doing. People who buy beach houses probably want them set up and ready to go."

This makes me feel even worse. Strangers living in *my* house. I try to push the idea from my mind as I paint over the gray boards.

"A white wedding cake is not as pure and offers less reason for celebration," Aunt Guin says, coming outside to look at the house.

"It's tastier though," Art counters.

"There are instances when that is debatable," Aunt Guin says.

"True," Art says, putting his brush down. He looks over at me, then climbs down the ladder. "I'm going to go do some work in the backyard," he says.

I know he's doing it to give us time to talk, but I have no intention of taking advantage of the opportunity. I'm feeling a little ripped off, giving so much to something only to have it taken away.

"I guess it's you and me, kid," she says, bouncing up the ladder to take Art's place. "Do you want to play a game?"

"No."

"How about Twenty Questions?" she asks, as cheery as ever.

"No! Don't you ever listen to what other people want?"

She looks at me like a wounded puppy, and then she smiles. "No games then."

We both continue painting. The late-August sun feels cold on my back as the afternoon drags on. The sun is taking longer to set than the entire summer has taken to pass. I barely even noticed that it was going.

Chapter Twenty-one

As the sky turns red, I ride my bike over to Connor's, where I am forced, once again, to watch the sci-fi channel, though it doesn't take much convincing anymore. As it turns out, it's nowhere near as painful as I thought it was going to be. Less painful than, say, Billy's martial arts movies. Not that I'll be going to conventions or dressing up like an alien any time soon, but over the summer I've actually begun to enjoy *some* of the shows.

Connor's mother, who is even larger than I pictured when he said she was too fat for the bicycle, brings our dinner—burgers and fries—into the TV room from the short-order kitchen in their store. She's a stern but friendly woman, though her height—over six feet—intimidated me at first.

She knocks Connor's feet off the coffee table and yells, "How many times have I told you?"

"Sorry, Mom," he says meekly.

"Can I get you anything else, dear?" she sweetly asks me.

"No, thank you," I tell her.

The short-order kitchen and the endless supply of candy from the store take their toll on me despite the physical labor on the house, the search for Moonlight Palace, the biking and Aunt Guin's endless salads and fruit plates. The steak on the first night was definitely a "special occasion" meal. On top of my universal weight gain, over the summer I start to develop, and Aunt Guin has to take me to buy my first bra.

"You're growing up," she says as proudly as if she'd raised me.

"I'm getting fat," I correct her as I try on ever-increasing sizes while looking into what I hope is a funhouse mirror.

"You'd have to put on another twenty pounds before you even approached plump."

She's right, *if* you go by health standards and *not* the anorexic vogue.

Aunt Guin never lets me put myself down in any way.

"Words shape our world," she always says. "They have their own energy—positive and negative—and you should always choose the positive. Always treat words with the respect they so richly deserve."

My physical change doesn't go unnoticed by Connor, who at least tries to be subtle, looking away when I catch him staring at my chest, which is more than I can say for his brother, who I've christened Mullet Boy.

Mullet Boy is three years older than Connor. He's already showing the effects of the short-order kitchen, but not as much as his "Monkey" or Monk, as Mullet Boy calls him. They both stare and stare at my chest, which is why I now wear Aunt Guin's jean jacket if I know they're going to be around.

Monk is the same age as Mullet Boy. He would be taller if he didn't slouch all the time, not wanting to show Mullet Boy up as he follows him around, repeating the last part of whatever Mullet Boy says.

I'd think Parrot would be a more appropriate name than Monkey if it weren't for the way his unusually long arms swing loosely at his sides, bringing his knuckles dangerously close to the ground.

They're always torturing Connor, calling him names, hitting him on the back of the head. Sometimes Monk will sit on him, which I'm sure falls into the cruel and unusual punishment category. I try to get Connor to tell his parents.

"What for? A three-day reprieve in return for an endless barrage of 'Tattletale, tattletale, tied to a bull's tale, when the bull begins to pee, you shall have a cup of tea,'" he says, making an idiotic face and putting on the stupidest voice ever. "Well, no tea for me, thank you very much."

"He doesn't really say that, does he?"

"Yes," Connor says, "he's done it since we were kids. He knows how much it bugs me so he keeps doing it."

"So don't let it bug you," I tell him before I can stop myself from echoing what I'd heard from so many clueless adults.

He shoots me an *easy for you to say* glare before turning

away. I get the feeling I'm not the first person to offer him this completely useless piece of advice.

Connor isn't big enough to be able to protect himself physically. He's got his father's build and metabolism—neither of them are the least bit affected by calories. It's quite annoying. Connor's dad is a little shorter than Connor, who's only about five foot six. His dad's very friendly, but also sort of mouse-like, maybe because his wife weighs twice as much as he does.

As Connor's mom leaves the TV room, she gives the dog, a big black lab that sits on the couch beside me, a little swat on the nose, which is making its way up to my plate.

"And I've told you about your begging enough times too," she tells the dog.

Connor's family has two dogs—the Lab, Fred, and a German shepherd named Barney—who bookend us on the couch. Barney's older and pays no attention to the food at all. But Fred puts his chin on my lap, staring up at me with his big sad brown eyes, which make me feel that I'm neglecting him by not sharing. I give him some of my fries to alleviate my guilt.

They also have three cats—Pebbles, Bam Bam and Gazoo—so the house is far from pristine. But there's a comfort and a freedom in the air that are stronger than the smells, which really aren't *that* bad. That is, of course, until Mullet Boy enters, with Monk a few steps behind.

"Hey," Mullet Boy says, reaching over and grabbing a handful of Connor's fries before he sits down.

"Hey," Monk says as he reaches for some of my fries. My scowl stops him and he retreats to just behind Mullet Boy's chair.

"What you girls doin'?" Mullet Boy drones.

"Yeah, you girls," Monk repeats.

"Discussing the laws of quantum physics and how they affect space and time. Care to weigh in on the subject?" I say. Television, you great teacher, you.

Mullet Boy stares blankly as Monk looks to him for guidance.

"Yeah and what do you do in the dunes?" he asks, staring at my chest.

"The dunes," Monk repeats, followed by a snorting laugh that reminds me of Martha. I picture Monk's hand sliding down the back of his droopy jeans and I'm completely put off my food. I set the plate down on the floor, and Fred pounces on the burger, quickly followed by Monk. They each get half, Monk's half being ripped from Fred's mouth.

My hands free, I pull my jacket closed and cross my arms. It doesn't stop Mullet Boy from staring. Monk's more interested in his burger.

"You probably build sand castles and play with Barbies," Mullet Boy continues.

"Barbies," Monk says.

"Shut up," Connor yells at his brother.

"Shut up," Monk repeats, too distracted by his burger to be able to keep track of who is saying what.

Mullet Boy gives him a dirty look. Then he punctuates the look with a quick punch to Monk's leg, giving him a charley horse and causing Monk to drop the rest of his burger, which Fred quickly snatches.

Monk swings at the dog, trying to pass the punishment along, but Fred's too quick for him, resuming his place beside me on the couch while looking at Monk with what I'm sure is a victory smile. Fred's panting takes on the rhythm of *nya nya nya nya nya*.

Mullet Boy jumps to his feet, pretends to launch himself at Connor, stops and then pretends to lunge again.

"We'll get ya," he says, then looks at me. "Both of ya."

He raises his eyebrows and smiles.

"Both of ya," Monk repeats, still holding his leg. Mullet Boy punches him in the arm. He winces but doesn't respond.

Mullet Boy saunters out of the room with Monk in hobbling tow.

Chapter Twenty-two

Every morning, Connor and I search for the lost dance hall. But we are no closer to finding it than we were at the beginning of the summer. It's our final week, so we're redoubling our efforts, while still making sure that we aren't followed by the not-so-dynamic duo and that our bikes are especially well hidden.

Aunt Guin and I haven't talked all week. I've done my best to avoid her. Art tries to talk to me, but I avoid him also. I still help out, but I work by myself. The furniture is coming today, and I don't want to be there when it arrives, so I get an extra early start and meet up with Connor on the dunes just after sunrise. He's managed to get hold of a couple of wide-brimmed Tilley hats and a couple of Tilley shirts—proper explorer gear for sand dunes. Connor has the afternoon off, and I have no intention of going back to see the house being decorated—with some of my ideas—to increase its profitability. With walking sticks in hand, we set off.

It's nearly noon when we hear it. All morning we've been carefully searching—sticking our walking sticks into the sand to see if they hit anything, hoping for that dull *clunk* you hear in the movies when a shovel hits a treasure chest or a coffin.

We take our quest to the bigger dunes that lie at the tip of the peninsula.

I sit with my feet in the water, a few meters from Connor, my walking stick by my side, trying to cool myself, when…

THUD, THUD.

"I think I found something," Connor yells excitedly.

He's digging into the dune with his hands. I leave the walking stick, run over to him and push both my hands into the dune.

"Dig, dig," he says, the sand filling in the hole as quickly as we try to empty it.

And then we hear another something.

"What are you girls doin'?"

"Yeah, you girls."

I turn around and see Mullet Boy and Monk. They leave a trail in the sand as they drag their way over to us, neither of them having the ambition to lift their feet when they walk.

Connor doesn't bother to turn around; he only lowers his head and shakes it. I stand up and walk a few meters to meet them.

"Leave us alone, Mullet Boy." It's the first time I've called him that to his face, and he doesn't seem to find it as amusing as I do.

He moves, pulling his right hand over his left shoulder like he's going to backhand me, but when the hand comes around, it grabs my shoulder and pushes me down onto the beach.

Connor gets up and runs to my defense, but Mullet Boy uses Connor's forward momentum against him, simply moving aside while sticking his foot out. He gives Connor a hard push on his back, which sends him tumbling to the ground near Monk, who promptly sits on Connor and washes his face with sand.

While Connor spits sand out of his mouth, Mullet Boy drives his fist into the dune where we were digging. With some struggle, he pulls out a piece of driftwood. Connor and I both sigh with disappointment.

"This what you were looking for?" he mocks.

"Looking for?"

Connor puts his forearm under his forehead, hiding his face.

"We're looking for Moonlight Palace," I say.

Connor looks up at me with a *what'd you tell them that for?* expression.

Mullet Boy laughs and Monk echoes it, without getting the joke.

"A fairy chasing a fairy tale," Mullet Boy says. "That's funny."

"Funny," Monk repeats.

"Be like you looking for a donkey," I say.

Mullet Boy looks at me, not understanding.

"Don't need to hear from the princess who lives with the circus act," he says, which brings me to my feet.

"Circus act," Monk mimics.

"I don't live with a circus act," I say.

"A woman who's a carpenter and a pasty-faced weirdo? Sounds like a circus act to me."

"Pasty face," Monk says, bringing my blood to a boil, as Aunt Milly would say.

Mullet Boy pulls out a Zippo lighter and starts playing with it, reminding me of Bam Bam's singed fur and Connor's remark about the cat's tail.

"Now," Mullet Boy says, staring at my chest. I don't have my jacket to shield myself with, "what do you want to do for fun, Monk?"

"For fun," Monk says, also staring at me.

Connor struggles hard to get out from under Monk's massive weight but to no avail.

I begin to shake with anger as Mullet Boy takes a step closer.

"Look, Monk, circus girl's trembling with excitement."

"Excitement," says Monk.

Mullet Boy gets a little closer. "Thinks it's her lucky day."

And with that, the past, the present and the future come together: my fear of them and my anger at them; my rage at my abandonment; the knowledge that you can do anything if you take it one microsecond at a time. I visualize what I'm about to do, seeing it clearly in my mind before making my first move, and then...

My foot hooks under the walking stick. With a quick kick it's in my hand, and with a fast swing it's between Mullet Boy's legs. As he hunches over I swing it again, taking him hard in the chin. He flies to the side, dropping face-first in the sand. I pirouette over him and bring the butt end of the stick into Monk's chest, sending him backward and freeing Connor, who goes for the other walking stick.

I stand sideways, legs apart, one arm stretched in front, the other holding the stick that's tucked into my armpit. In this crouching tiger stance, I look Monk dead in the eyes.

"You are not ready for the fight you have started," I say. "Leave now or meet a most painful demise."

People really do underestimate the educational value of movies and television.

"Yeah," Connor says.

"Demise?" Monk says, turning to Mullet Boy—who's already halfway up the dune.

"Wait," Monk yells after him, scrambling to his feet and waddling as fast as he can to get back into position behind Mullet Boy.

"I'll get you for this, Connor," Mullet Boy yells from the safety of the dune's crown.

"Do, and everyone will know that you got your butt kicked—by a girl!" Connor yells back.

"Yeah!" Mullet Boy shouts. "Well…you're lucky."

I raise my stick and they disappear over the top.

"That was awesome," Connor says. I start to cry.

"What's wrong?" Connor asks. "We won."

I don't know what's wrong. I just know I can't stop crying. I drop to my knees and Connor puts his arm awkwardly around me. I fall into his chest and I cry and cry.

Chapter Twenty-three

The desire to find Moonlight Palace has been knocked out of me, and I tell Connor that I'm willing to admit defeat. He reluctantly agrees that conceding failure is the wisest course of action. Aunt Guin would not approve.

The disappointment, the battle and my tears have taken the best out of us and we make our way to a shady area at the top of the last dune at the tip of the peninsula. We sit there, staring out over the lake, letting its calmness sink into us. I have no sense of time passing or of there being a world outside of this one—sand, water, trees, gulls, me and Connor. Looking at the clear blue sky, I think that heaven must be a lot like this place—without Mullet Boy and Monk, of course— and I can almost understand why Mom wanted to go there.

But she didn't want to go, she didn't want to leave me, she had no choice. I don't know if that makes me feel better or worse.

I lie down and Connor lies quietly beside me as the future starts creeping toward us.

"I don't want to leave," I confess.

Connor doesn't say anything in reply. He just reaches over, grabs my hand and gives it a squeeze. I let him; I even squeeze back, and then I drift into sleep.

When Connor wakes me up, the sun is gone, replaced by a full moon that's almost as bright.

"Why didn't you wake me sooner?" I ask.

"I fell asleep too," he tells me. "We'd better take the trail through the woods," he adds, collecting our things.

I look at the forest, which doesn't seem at all welcoming at night, no matter how bright the moon.

"You sure?"

"It'll cut our travel time in half," he states.

The forest becomes more sinister the farther in we venture. Dancing evening shadows make room for their deadly, older, larger and darker siblings. The black, distorted reflections of trees cover large patches of the forest floor, blocking the silver blue moonlight that offers our only source of light or comfort.

The trees work together, blending one shadow into the next, trying to keep us in eternal darkness. I want to run from the creatures that inhabit this forest and move all around me.

Each twig-snap's echo is sustained. The trees play catch with the sounds, and I want to cover my ears, but I fear it would make it far too easy for one of the demons to sneak up on me. I can see Fanny staring into a crystal ball, controlling all the creatures of the night, cackling as she commands them to attack.

I look to the sky, hoping to see Aunt Guin coming to the rescue, descending in a pink dress with a magic wand, encapsulated in a silver blue moonlit bubble. I resist the urge to tap my heels together and say "There's no place like home" over and over again. At the very least, it would drown out the scurrying sounds that surround us.

"How much farther?" I say, unsettled by the tremble in my voice.

"Not far." I'm further unsettled by the tremble in *his* voice and downright scared by the uncertainty.

I look down at my feet, hoping to see ruby slippers, but instead I see that we're no longer on the path.

"Where's the trail?" I ask.

Connor looks down and then quickly up again and increases his pace.

"Don't worry," he says, which of course means that there's something to worry about.

"Please tell me you know the way."

"Yeah," he replies, even less convincingly than before.

"Connor?"

"I know the way in the daytime...sort of." He tries to reassure me. "But I—I usually avoid the forest at night."

"Didn't need to hear that," I tell him.

"Wait," he says, stopping.

"What?" I ask nervously.

"I think I see something."

"What?" I ask more nervously.

"Light," he replies. "An opening or an ending."

Chapter Twenty-four

I bring my face up next to Connor's. In the near distance, the darkness retreats into a pale blue that glistens like a swimming pool in the night. We push forward and, escaping the forest, emerge into an opening illuminated by cascading moonlight. On the far side are the remains of a large stone fireplace. As we walk toward it, the ground beneath our feet changes texture, and I look down to see that we're standing on a marble dance floor.

"This is it," I say.

"What?" he asks, still nervous.

"Moonlight Palace."

"But it's not buried," he says.

Before the words even leave his mouth, sand descends upon us as gently as a Christmas Eve snowfall.

"It is," I say as I watch each grain grab the moonlight to reveal a different moment in time. "And it isn't. It depends on which moment you're in. Moonlight Palace doesn't just take you back to its heyday; it takes you anywhere you want to go. You just have to choose."

I turn to the left and see the water on the other side of a line of trees whose tops lean toward each other like dancers bowing to their partners at the end of a waltz. The shapes in between the trees form high-pointed ballroom windows, and the apparition of a chandelier of stars floats above us.

The marble floor catches the falling moonlight and glows from its touch. Bathed in the blue, I feel the light wrap itself around me, touching every part of me at the same time, holding me, comforting me.

I can smell the lake and the evergreens; their scents twirl around us, mixing with the fragrance of wild flowers floating through air so clean you'd think it had just been polished by snow. It's as if the seasons all came together to create one intoxicating fragrance.

Connor and I look at each other and smile.

He asks me to dance by bowing and extending his hand like a true nobleman. I take it and I look at him. The reflection in his eyes is one I barely recognize.

I like who I see when I see myself in his eyes.

This time I kiss him. My first real kiss because it's not to forget but to remember. My body tingles with life, and time disappears.

Through a window I see the stars turn the black forest into a yellow wood.

We'll find our way, I say to myself, by making our own path. But not just yet.

"It's strange," I say.

"Don't question it," Connor tells me.

"That's not what I mean," I reply.

"What, then?"

"When you know you have the power to go anywhere and do anything, you're happy just to dance."

Together we sway to the sounds of the Moonlight Palace Orchestra. From behind the piano, Mom looks up, and an approving smile dawns on her rosy face.

Chapter Twenty-five

When I get home, I run straight to the washroom. I'm bursting. While enjoying the great release, I also take pleasure in seeing how the bathroom has changed since that first night. A tall cabinet stands on the multicolored spiral-tiled floor.

Moonlight illuminates the harp in the center of the stained glass window. In the door's frosted glass, I spot a flickering yellow light.

Exiting the bathroom, I look into the living room where Aunt Guin sits in a brown leather chair by the fire that burns under a cherrywood mantel.

"Come in," she says. I make my way past the paintings and the framed *Wizard of Oz* poster, admiring the grand piano before I sit across from Aunt Guin on the matching leather couch.

"What do you think?" she asks.

"It's just as I imagined," I reply.

"There's magic down here. Your grandparents used to bring us up to the beach every year. Your mom was eleven the last time we came; I was seventeen."

She stops talking, gets up, walks over to the fireplace and stokes the fire. I want to tell her about Moonlight Palace. I want to apologize for how I've behaved, but the flames give Aunt Guin a mournful look that stops me from saying anything.

I've never seen Aunt Guin look unhappy, and I want to say something that will make her happy again, but I see that she isn't finished speaking, so I wait.

"Things changed after that. I went off to university and came home less and less until finally, when your mom was about sixteen, I stopped coming altogether. Your grandparents didn't approve of how I chose to live my life, but in all fairness, I didn't give them much of a chance to get used to it. I didn't even go to their funerals, and I wasn't going to go to your mom's. I was hiding in the park when I saw you talking to the ants. I knew at a glance who you were."

"Didn't you love your family?" I ask.

"I loved them very much, especially your mom. But I try to avoid unhappy situations, never staying in a place long enough to get attached, taking each moment on its own. If nothing ever gets you down, you can fly as high and as far as you wish," she says. Her voice lacks conviction.

"But when you fall, you've got nowhere to land," I say.
She sighs.

"I thought it best not to depend on anyone. That way they can't let you down when you need them the most, which is when they always go." Her words have a familiar ring, which stings me a little. "I've missed out on a lot, not getting to know you before now, just seeing how much you've changed over the summer. I'm glad I finally got that chance."

"Why are you talking like you're leaving?"

She smiles and gives me a hug and a kiss on the forehead.

"I just wanted to let you know that I'm honored to have met you. Now go to bed. You've got a big day tomorrow."

"What's tomorrow?"

"It's important to ask questions, and you should never stop doing that. Except right now."

She smiles again and the sparkle returns, but not as brightly as before.

"Go upstairs," she says. "There's a bed waiting for you."

I turn on the light in my room and burst out laughing at the mural she's painted on the wall. It's a mermaid with my face and hair, tangled in seaweed. She's holding a pocket watch that has no face at all and only a second hand. I climb into bed and dream of all that was and all that will be, while never forgetting where I am.

Chapter Twenty-six

I'm awoken by the smell of bacon. I throw on my swimsuit and look out at the beach. The welcoming sun, whose
beams playfully bounce off the rippling lake, calls for me to
come and join in the games. I pull shorts and a T-shirt over
my swimsuit and run down the stairs. Looking out front to
see if Connor's stopped by, I notice that Art's van is gone.

"Aunt Guin," I say as I run into the kitchen, where I see
that it's real bacon frying in the pan. "Aunt Guin?"

The side door opens and I turn to see...

"Dad?"

"J!" Billy yells, appearing from behind Dad's legs. He runs
at me full steam, wrapping his little arms around my legs.

"Hey, buddy!" I say, bending down and giving him a big
hug in return.

"How was your summer?" Dad asks, like he *hadn't* talked
to me every week on the phone.

"Fine," I say, to humor him. "Where's Aunt Guin?"

"She had to go. She called me last night to ask if I could come up and get you."

"Why?"

"That's your Aunt Guin," he says in a *par for the course* way.

Then a terrible thought creeps in. "Did Fanny come with you?"

"No," he says dismissively.

"A house didn't land on her, did it?" I say before I can stop myself. I see a little smile on his face, but only for a second. Then it's gone.

"I'm sorry," I say. "I shouldn't have said that."

"Billy," Dad says, "can you go in the other room?"

"But there's no TV," Billy says.

"You can play your Game Boy."

"Okay," Billy replies.

After Billy leaves the room, I turn to Dad and speak before he has a chance to lecture.

"I'm sorry for the way I acted at the funeral and after. I…"

"No, J, I'm the one who should be apologizing. I'm your father. I should have been there for you and I wasn't."

"Dad, you were…"

"I was nothing…that's the problem. But that's going to change." He takes a deep, strengthening breath. "I loved your mom very much. I still do." I step toward him and he grabs hold of me and gives me a hug, the biggest I've ever gotten from anyone. Then he lets go and quickly turns away.

"Let's have some breakfast," he says. "Billy!"

After breakfast I help Dad with the dishes.

"Mind if I go for a walk on the beach before we go?" I ask.

"No rush," he replies. "I thought we might stay the weekend."

"That'd be great," I say. "Mind if I go on the beach anyway?"

"Not in the least."

"Want to come?" I ask him.

"Maybe later."

"Can I come?" Billy asks, staring at his Game Boy.

"Sure, but you have to leave your Game Boy here."

"Okay," he says, jumping off his chair.

"You are awfully obliging, young sir," I tell him.

"What's that mean?" he asks.

"It means you're cool and I'm happy you're here."

"I'm happy I'm here too," he tells me, running out ahead.

Just before I exit, Dad yells, "Wait!" He comes to the door and hands me a letter. "Your Aunt Guinevere left you this."

"Thanks," I say. "Dad, why did Mom never tell me about Aunt Guin?"

"She was worried you'd want to get to know her and that you'd end up getting hurt when she eventually and inevitably stopped contacting you."

"And what do you think?" I ask, wondering why he let me spend the summer with her if she's so dangerous.

He lowers his head for a moment, then looks at me again. "Aunt Milly says you have to take the good with the bad, and she's right. Pain's a part of life. If you avoid it, you miss out on some of the best parts."

"Dad?" I say.

"Yeah?"

"I'm not hurt, not really."

"I know," he says. "You're very resilient."

"Dad?" I say.

"Yeah."

"I love you."

He smiles.

"J?"

"Yeah?"

"I love you too."

I smile.

Chapter Twenty-seven

At the top of the dunes I look at the house, which shines proudly, showing off its fresh white paint and its new green shutters. I sit and open the letter from Aunt Guin.

Art says good-bye.
I'm no good at good-byes.
I'm keeping the house.
See you next summer.
Love,
Aunt Guin

I fold the letter and put it in my pocket. I look down at the clear blue water and up at the clear blue heavens and smile. I let the sand form around me while Billy rolls down the dune, climbs to the top and rolls back down again. I close my eyes and feel the sun's warmth on my face. I'm happy it's there to watch over me.

I see Mom's smiling face, her skin pink and perfect. I hear her laugh and feel her arms around me. I'm in the moment, but if time is an illusion, then all that came before and all that comes after, everyone I've ever loved or will love, is here with me. All things happen simultaneously, but like ultraviolet light and the wind, our perceptions are just too limited to see them. All we can do is feel their effect and know that they're there.

"J," Billy yells.

I straighten up to see what he wants and get hit in the back of the head.

"Agghh!" Connor screams.

"Cool," Billy says.